# ALFIE'S ADVENTURES

## Book 1

## Gerald Howe

Pen Press Publishers Ltd

First published in Great Britain
Pen Press Publishers Ltd
39-41 North Road
London N7 9DP

ISBN 1-905203-19-5

Printed and bound in Great Britain

Cover design by Jacqueline Abromeit
Illustrations by Channimation

## About the Author

Gerald Howe was born in Bedford in 1954 to a family of farmers and cattle dealers. He went to Bedford Modern School and represented England at rowing.

Happily married to Jacqueline since 1976, the couple have two sons, Mathew and Henry, and a black Labrador called Eddie!

Gerald has worked at various airports including Heathrow where he looked after the in-flight catering of Qantas, Gulf Air and TWA Airlines. He later became a restaurateur and then a hotelier, and moved to Jersey in the Channel Islands in 1988.

Though actively involved in an electronics business in Bedford, in his spare time he sat down at his computer and started to write the Alfie stories . . . which he hopes will give children a sense of adventure and an interest in reading.

## Foreword

Calling all potential heroes!

Roman emperors, jungle explorers, maps to find hidden treasures and lost cities and plans to save the Earth from pollution – exactly what you wouldn't expect to find on board a Virgin flight.

But look within these pages to join Alfie and his faithful dog Eddie as they time travel around the world to different places and times, being an action hero in the past, present and future.

Best of all, Alfie's night-time adventures seem to be giving him heroic powers during the day as he catches criminals, saves a man from drowning and to top it all, beats the school bully at his own game.

So, settle back into your Virgin seat AS IT MAY BE WORTH YOUR WHILE TO LEARN what you would do if…

… you were imprisoned in the hold of your own ship

… the train track ahead of you has been blown up by bandits

… you were beaten at conkers by a girl

… you came face to face with the Abominable Snowman

.. you were rewarded for finding a horde of Roman coins

Read on to find out how to be a hero and enjoy!

Best Wishes

Gerald Howe

PS. See how smart you are. Every picture has a Virgin "V" hidden within it. Can you find them all?

# ALFIE'S ADVENTURES

## Book 1

# Chapter One: The bed & the Salty Duck

"Alfie, Alfie, ALFRED HENRY NELSON, WILL YOU COME IN NOW!" called his mother standing in the doorway.

Alfie reluctantly turned and trudged into the house. Bedtime was boring! Why couldn't he stay up and play in the garden with his black Labrador dog, Eddie, and the hard rubber ball? Eddie followed him in, echoing Alfie's slumped walk, and sat beside him with the ball in his mouth. He too seemed to go "Humph", as he didn't like to come in either.

But it was Alfie's bedtime and his mother marched him up the stairs to the bedroom. "Come on," she said. "Get those dirty clothes off so I can put them in the washer. Hurry up as it's getting late and you need some sleep… so you can grow big and strong."

Why does she always say that? thought Alfie, as he wriggled into his pyjamas and went to brush his teeth. The toothpaste tube was alive as he squeezed the paste out into a giant worm on his brush and he brushed it away on his own fangs before drowning it down the plughole.

"And remember, you have a new bed to sleep in tonight!" his mother reminded him as she fussed around him in the bathroom.

Alfie brightened and stopped playing with the toothpaste. He had quite forgotten about his new bed. Not a shop-bought new bed, but a present to Alfie from his Grampy who was an antique collector and traveller, and a fascinating old character. He had recently shipped the bed back from one of his visits to Bombay.

A hotel he had stayed in was full, except for a tiny room in the farthest reaches of the hotel. The bed in it was too small but, Grampy HAD no choice than to take what he was offered. That night, he was so comfortable and he had such dreams! The next day the hotel owner told him that the bed had chosen him! This mysterious man said that he must buy the ornate bed; he was most insistent and sold it to him very cheaply. Grampy, being a collector, was only too keen to comply and had the bed shipped back to England for his grandson.

Alfie loved the bed immediately. Both ends of the bed had dark wooden slats, and on each corner was an ornate post topped with temptingly smooth round spheres. Upon closer investigation, Alfie noticed that the carvings on the bed posts were comprised of letters and numbers. A far more exciting bed than his last one!

He drew the curtains tight shut and looked under the bed and in the wardrobe before pulling the duvet up to his nose and sinking down into the soft mattress and pillows which seemed to whisper to him, saying, "Go to sleep, Alfie, and rest your weary head. You've had a busy, busy day, little man."

Alfie's mum looked in five minutes later and gave him a goodnight kiss on his forehead. He was fast asleep and Eddie, his faithful companion, was on guard in his basket on the floor beside him. (Really the dog was asleep too!) His legs were twitching as he dreamed of chasing rabbits on the heath, he even dreamed that one day he might catch one and give it a big lick.

Alfie was dreaming now too and his bed had turned into a large old sailing ship called *The Labrador*, with high masts and a crew bustling about him. Of course Alfie was the captain. He stood on the quarter deck at the stern of the boat and he could feel its gentle rocking and the creaking of timber as the

ship sailed along on the light warm wind of the Caribbean.

He looked up at the top of the mast as the sailor in the crow's-nest on lookout duty shouted out, "Captain! Captain! Warship off the starboard beam. I think it's a pirate!"

Captain Alfie scanned the sea with his polished brass telescope and saw the warship; it was a pirate alright. He could see the Jolly Roger Skull and Crossbones flag fluttering from the top mast. As the pirate ship neared he could see the brass nameplate and the large carved duck figurehead on the bow. It was the scourge of the Seven Seas, *The Salty Duck* with its Captain Barnacle Green. The two captains had crossed cutlasses before – they had fought to a draw and both had had to retreat to save their damaged ships.

Captain Alfie shouted to his crew to 'prepare to come about' and his bugler told the ship to 'prepare for war'. The cannon doors were opened on the side of the ship and the loaded cannons were primed with gunpowder and loaded with cannon balls ready for action.

The two ships passed by each other barely two hundred yards apart and Alfie could see Barnacle Green grinning at him from *The Salty Duck's* deck, revealing his black teeth.

The two captains shouted "Fire" at the same time and both ships shook from the cannon blast and there were huge clouds of white smoke billowing from the sides of the ship.

There was a loud crack and the forward mast of *The Labrador* fell down on the deck; men were covered in rope and rigging and a small fire had started on the bows. Sailors rushed with buckets of water and dowsed the flames.

*The Salty Duck* sheared away and went round to attack again. Barnacle Green was grinning now, and he was going to finish his score with that Captain Alfie Henry Nelson, who was the pride of the King's fleet.

The situation looked desperate on *The Labrador* but Captain Alfie had a plan. He remembered that one day when he was walking by a lake he threw a stone at a rock some distance from the shore as hard as he could but he couldn't get to within twenty feet of it. He then tried to skim a stone at it and after bouncing twice it hit the rock with a bang. He wondered if he could use this trick to give his gunners a range advantage.

He ordered his cannons' sights to be lowered to a flat angle with the water and when *The Salty Duck* was normally too far away to hit, he ordered them to fire. The crew of *The Labrador* thought he was mad to fire so early, but then they saw the cannon balls bounce off the water and smash into the side of *The Salty Duck* below the water line.

There was jubilation on *The Labrador* as *The Salty Duck* started to lean over and got lower in the water; she was sinking fast and Captain Barnacle Green was waving a white flag of surrender. He wasn't laughing now.

Captain Alfie brought *The Labrador* alongside the sinking ship and took *The Salty Duck's* crew prisoner and was presented the captain's sword as a sign of his surrender. Barnacle Green agreed on his honour to not cause any trouble and Captain Alfie invited him to dine with him before putting *The Labrador* into Trinidad for repairs. When they docked, the prisoners walked down the gangplank and into jail for their piracy. Loud cheers greeted Captain Alfie as the Governor of Trinidad presented him with a large reward for capturing the evil Barnacle Green and freeing the Seven Seas from such a villainous pirate.

Alfie was tired after all this excitement and retired to his bunk on board and was soon fast asleep.

He awoke with a rather wet lick from Eddie, to tell him it was time to get up. The sun was streaming through a gap in the curtains.

Alfie rubbed his eyes and said, "So it was all a dream, but it seemed so real."

He rolled over to get out of bed when he felt something

hard under his pillow. Lifting it up he found a cutlass in a scabbard engraved on the blade with the name CAPTAIN BARNACLE GREEN.

# Chapter Two: X marks the spot?

Alfie couldn't wait for school to finish, even though it was his favourite class – Geography. The clock seemed to tick slower than usual; outside it was grey, cloudy and lightly raining.

Alfie wanted to get home and examine the Captain's sword that he had found under his pillow when he had woken up that morning. He had just been going to look at it when his father had told him to hurry up for school as he was giving him a lift on his way to work in town.

He hid the sword under the bed in a pull-out drawer, put on his cap and school blazer and dashed down the stairs to jump in the car with his dad. His dad asked him if he was alright after they had been travelling for more than five minutes without Alfie saying a word. Alfie had been deep in thought about the sword and his adventure the night before. But he didn't think his dad would understand, so he told him that he was thinking about his classes and his friend's birthday party at the weekend.

The school bell rang for the end of school and Alfie almost broke the record for the twenty yard sprint to the cloakroom to get his coat and cap. His teacher, Mrs Allendale, told him to slow down but he had already disappeared into the throng of children, happy that the important task of having an education had finished for the day.

Alfie stood by the school gates and was pleased to see his mother striding towards him with Eddie the Labrador on his lead. He was soon beside them and, as the dog had come too, they went home via the park. The rain had stopped and the sun tried to break through the gloom. They let Eddie off the lead and he ran around the park sniffing at each tree like his nose was a vacuum cleaner. It was just a short walk today. They left the park with Eddie safely on his lead after a small struggle as he had been playing excitedly with a small white Scottie dog called Hamish. Eddie saw Hamish almost every day but he still hated to leave him – they were mates!

Alfie understood that, but he was in a hurry to get home. They all rounded the corner and were in Acacia Drive. Nearly there, thought Alfie, as he went in front and opened the garden gate for his mother and Eddie to go in first.

"Thank you," said his mother, "what a proper little gentleman you are!" She always says that, thought Alfie, as he followed her into the kitchen for his tea. He washed his hands to get off the dark blue ink that he was supposed to put on the paper in writing classes but seemed to soak onto his fingers at every opportunity.

He sat at the table and ate his tea (closely assisted by Eddie the canine dustbin on legs, no treats refused!). Alfie drank a big glass of milk and put the glass and dishes on the sink for his mother to wash.

Alfie's mother had put the television on for him to watch the children's programmes but he went straight up to his room. He quietly closed the door behind him and went to the bed's drawer to make sure that the sword was really there. To his delight he pulled it out and laid it on top of the bed. He marvelled at it and examined it closely; the engraving said CAPTAIN BARNACLE GREEN. The hilt was covered in golden woven metal threads with a big gold tassel hanging from it. It was most definitely not a dream. Alfie couldn't understand how it had all happened but he was glad it had. He decided to clean it and put it away carefully.

He was cleaning the top part of the sword's handle when he noticed that there was a big knob which was a little loose. He grasped it tightly and twisted it; it came off and revealed a small piece of paper, rolled up tightly and hidden in the hilt. As he unrolled it Alfie saw that it was a tiny map. He spread it on his chest of drawers. It was so small that the writing was hard to read; Alfie got a magnifying glass and proceeded to inspect it. At the top it simply said Tortuga and the shape of an island was drawn underneath it with a few place names and a big black cross on the left hand side, next to Mango Creek swamp. Beside the cross was a name – Captain Henry Morgan.

Suddenly he heard footsteps coming up the stairs. It was his mother to put him to bed – could it really be that late, he thought as he dashed to hide his treasures away from the sight of a mother who had a detective type of mind and could read him like an open book.

His mother played with him as he got ready to go to bed and soon he was tucked up in the dreamboat bed with Eddie keeping him company. The dog loved any excuse to get warm, curl up and go to sleep.

*

The clouds of sleep turned into sea breezes and warm sunshine as Captain Alfie walked the decks of *The Labrador*. The sails billowed and the seabirds screeched as they weighed anchor and set off to the island of Tortuga.

Captain Alfie called all the officers into his cabin for a briefing on the mission he had in mind. He showed them the map and they consulted an admiralty chart of the island of Tortuga. The officers were excited to see the map, and particularly the name of Captain Henry Morgan. Morgan had used Tortuga as his base in 1680. He was an English buccaneering pirate and had used the island many times to split his plunder with his pirate crews.

One of those henchmen had been Captain Barnacle Green. So it was possible that this was a map to the long lost hoard of buried treasure that had disappeared one day when Morgan left the fort at Tortuga with sixteen men laden down with treasure chests and shovels. Morgan sailed off just as the sun was dawning, arriving back two days later - and the sixteen men were never seen again. He even joked that he had left them on guard with his treasure. Many men tried to find the treasure but all were unsuccessful.

Could Captain Alfie really have found the map which would lead to the buried treasure? "Only one way to find out," he said to his men. "Let's go and look… anyway, Tortuga's on our way back to Blighty." (That's Britain in seafarers' talk.) The time passed at sea with sailors singing and dancing to shanties and all the hustle and bustle of life on one of His Majesty's ships.

The weather had changed as they neared Tortuga's coast and a squall meant that they had to head for the safety of the main harbour. They battled the storm, and the crew were relieved when they could hear the clattering of the anchor being dropped in the harbour.

The wind howled all that night and the rain fell like buckets of water being poured out onto the ship's decks. The sailors were all tucked up in their hammocks and were gently swaying below decks.

The next day all was calm again, the harbour with its roughly built little houses and shelters looking scrubbed clean from the storm. The sky was blue, the palm trees swayed gently and the beaches looked serene, as if the storm hadn't even happened. Captain Alfie started ordering his men to tidy the ship and, whilst they did this, he and two officers went ashore to buy provisions and order water to be loaded up on the ship for the long journey home. This took all day and soon all was ship-shape and Bristol fashion.

Alfie went into The Blue Parrot tavern for a well earned drink with his officers and were served glasses of hot milk by a lady who looked like his mother. They resolved to start the search for the treasure the following day.

Leaving a trusted officer in charge, Captain Alfie and some of his crew set out to follow the map's directions.

They headed into the jungle that surrounded the port, and soon they had penetrated deep into the trees where the sunlight barely filtered down to the forest floor. The brave men followed their captain, with his small, trusty compass pointing the way towards the cross and Mango Creek swamp. They could hear the sounds of the jungle all around them. Parrots shrieked and wild pigs squealed as they were disturbed by the band of adventurers. Although none of the men admitted it, they were each a little bit nervous.

They all froze as a giant snake slithered by with a loud hiss. This was getting a bit dangerous, Captain Alfie thought, but they decided to go on as this mission might solve the mystery of the disappearing men and treasures.

The jungle became so dense that soon they were cutting their way through with machetes. It was steamy and humid in the jungle, and soon everyone was really hot and thirsty. They were all relieved when they finally arrived at a clearing with a waterfall. A small cheer went up when Captain Alfie decided it would be a good place to stop for a rest and a drink.

After a quick refresh, Captain Alfie checked his bearings and he suddenly realised that off to his left was Mango Swamp. "We're here!" he exclaimed and suddenly all thought of rest was gone. They laid the map out and started to look for landmarks. They noticed the waterfall was marked, as was a large palm tree which leaned over alarmingly.

The cross on the map looked like it was around the waterfall. They had brought shovels with them and they started to dig.

An hour later a very hot, tired and disappointed Captain Alfie sat down by the side of the giant hole that he and his men had dug, without finding anything.

"Perhaps someone else has already found it," he said disappointed. "What a lot of hard word for nothing! Still, as we are all dirty from the dig, let's have a swim and cool off." Captain Alfie stripped off and jumped into the inviting cool clear water, leaving a muddy slick behind him as the dirt came off. Alfie began to feel a bit better and swam up and down the pool at the bottom of the waterfall. Some of his crew didn't like the thought of clean and water, so they stayed by the side of the pool cooking some food over an open fire.

Captain Alfie was about to get out of the water when he noticed a small glint at the bottom of the pool. He held his breath and dived down to the bottom and brought the small object to the surface. He couldn't believe his eyes – it was a solid gold coin, a piece of eight! "Look, Look," he cried, as his men gathered round to see. Even the dirty unwashed men who hated the thought of being clean now jumped into the water and started diving to the bottom. Soon they had recovered twenty pieces of eight. They looked but could find no more.

They were about to go back to the ship when Captain Alfie had an idea – he remembered a book he'd read where the hero hid from the baddies by hiding in a space beneath the falling water of a waterfall. He wondered – could there be a cave behind the falling water?

He skirted the side of the waterfall and looked into the falling water, and sure enough he could see a space. He tied himself to a rope and got his crew to hold it while he climbed up under the downpour. Success! He found an open area large enough to climb into and it was sloping gently upwards so only the bottom part was wet. He called back down to his men to confirm he had found a cave, and a couple of the men started climbing up the rope behind him.

He went into the cave, but it was so big, deep and dark that he couldn't see much at all.

Luckily he had a steel and tinderbox in his pocket. He felt around and found a piece of cloth on the floor with a stick. He wrapped the cloth around the stick and started a fire with his tinderbox. The crew joined him as the cloth caught alight. They were suddenly struck dumb at the sight that met their eyes. They were surrounded by chests with big brass bands around them that glinted in the torchlight. They could scarcely breathe as Captain Alfie forced open one of the chests. It was filled with gold, rubies and pearls, with silver plates and goblets in the others.

There were so many treasures that the crew took three days fetching and loading the treasure onto *The Labrador*. They tried to conceal what they had by putting the treasure into barrels but the chatter all around the dock was that they had found the long lost treasure of Captain Henry Morgan.

Captain Alfie was glad to sail from Tortuga and head for England and home. He walked the decks until dark and went to his hammock.

*

Alfie was woken gently by his mother and Eddie; it was time to get up and what had he been mumbling in his sleep just before she woke him up? She said "It sounded like 'Pirates off the port bow'. I wonder what adventures you have been dreaming about." His mother laughed gently.

But as she went out of the bedroom, Alfie felt under his pillow and he was not surprised to find a gold coin dated 1680. He was only sorry that it was just one!

# Chapter Three: The power of prayer

Today was Saturday, so there was no school. Alfie still had to move as it was time for his mother to go to her part-time job in the beachside café at Sandcastle Bay, which was about three miles away. Alfie always went with her if it was a nice day. He put on his sun hat and did up his seat belt in the car. Eddie liked the beach as well so he came too. They parked up on the gravel car park and Alfie and Eddie ran off to explore the rock pools on the beach. The sand was warm between his barefoot toes and the seaweed popped as he stood on it. He could see his mum behind the counter selling bacon sandwiches with hot tea or coffee. She had made it a rule for him not to wander out of sight and especially not to speak to strangers. He always obeyed because he knew she would stop him playing in the rockpools if he ever ventured out of sight. And this was so much fun.

Eddie was woofing at a crab in a pool of water. The dog had got its front legs stretched out with its hair stood up on his back and was backing away trying to make out it was brave, but Alfie knew he was just a big girl's blouse – which was what his dad called him if ever he acted chicken. Alfie tried to get the crab but it sank under the water and hid beneath a rock. Alfie knew that his dad loved to eat crab and salad so he resolved to catch it if he could.

He ran to his mother at the café and asked her for some bacon rinds and a piece of string, which she gave him. He was just leaving when Grace, the café owner's daughter (who

Alfie thought was alright for a girl!) asked if she could come and play too.

They went to the rock pool to hunt for the crab. Alfie tied the bits of bacon rind to the string and lowered it into the pool. He wiggled the string and within a minute the bait was being pulled at by the crab. Alfie gently tugged the string and lifted it out of the pool. The greedy crab came with it and Alfie lowered it into his sand bucket. The crab started snapping with its claws as Alfie and Grace ran to her dad (the café chef) with the bucket. Alfie wanted him to cook it for his dad but Grace's dad said it was too small and let it go.

Alfie, Grace and Eddie started to play on the beach. Eddie dug holes whilst Alfie and Grace built castles beside them. The day passed amazingly quickly, as it always does when you're having fun, and soon it was time for the café to close and for them to go home.

Alfie had his tea and then a bath before he went to bed. Saturday nights were when his dad read him a story. Tonight was a tale of knights in armour and damsels in distress, which Alfie loved. But tonight, Alfie felt his eyelids getting heavier and heavier; his pillow felt so soft that it only took ten minutes of reading and he was fast asleep.

*

Captain Alfie awoke with something cold sticking into his ribs; it was a pirate's pistol and a tough looking pirate with an eye patch was holding it. "Get up," he said. "The ship is ours and we want Captain Morgan's treasure."

Captain Alfie's mind was racing – how could these pirates have taken his ship under sail at night without a fight or a warning? His hands were tied behind him and he was marched out on deck and into the warm, damp early morning air.

"Good morning, Captain Alfie," boomed a big deep voice.

Captain Alfie looked up to see a medium height round ball of a man with a long red beard. It was Redbeard, the Pirate King.

Alfie looked around the deck and saw that all his men, (except the new recruit from Tortuga) were locked in the ship's hold.

Alfie realized that this new recruit was a pirate. He had allowed the pirates on board after locking the crew in the hold and knocking out the helmsman. He felt stupid at being captured so easily with such a valuable cargo on board.

Redbeard the Pirate King ordered that Captain Alfie and his men be put into the hold, whilst he had some breakfast and before the entertainment of a plank walk for *The Labrador's* captain.

The men crowded round Captain Alfie, hoping that he would have a plan to get them out of this fix. Captain Alfie did have a plan! For inside the hold that he and his men were imprisoned, contained the barrels of treasure and barrels of gunpowder. Their captors didn't realise this as they both looked the same! Captain Alfie ordered that the treasure be taken out of one barrel and then he opened up a gunpowder barrel. He took out one third of the gunpowder and filled the barrel to the top with treasure. His men did this to the other barrels and they hid the balance of treasure barrels in the powder room. They had to work quickly and quietly, operating as a great team. Each of the barrels then had a small fuse laid in the crack of the wooden lids and was passed through a candle which was stuck on the lid as if to light the hold.

After breakfast the Pirate King decided that *The Labrador's* crew should carry the heavy treasure barrels into the hold of his ship. Captain Alfie's plan was working.

Indeed he found it hard not to grin when one of his men asked that the candles on the barrels be lighted so that they could see where to stow them in the pirate ship's hold.

The candles were lit, the barrels were stowed in the hold and as *The Labrador's* crew came out they 'unfortunately' forgot to put out the candles.

Redbeard pointed to Captain Alfie and beckoned him towards the plank which stretched out over the sea from the pirate ship's side. A cutlass poked him in the back and he was told to walk the plank. He slowly walked along the plank and stopped to glance down. There were sharks circling the boat, waiting for him after the pirates had tipped the remains of their breakfast into the sea.

"Come on, jump," said the pirates, "and feed the fishes," they laughed. Stalling for time while the candles burned, Captain Alfie asked that he be allowed to lead his men in one last prayer before his life was ended.

"Not unreasonable," said the Pirate King, "but do get on with it!"

Captain Alfie had been counting in his head and he thought that the candles would be nearly burnt through to the fuses by now. He told his men to get on their knees and bow their heads as he led them in The Lord's Prayer. The heathen pirates were all still stood up mainly on the deck of their own ship.

Captain Alfie got to the bit about "Deliver us from evil..." when the hold of the pirate ship exploded and blew the side of the ship out. Captain Alfie's crew were waiting and they seized the few remaining pirates who were shocked and dazed by what had happened. The pirate ship was sinking fast. The ropes joining her to *The Labrador* were cut and she sank.

Captain Alfie ordered the Pirate King and his men be put into irons and a course set for Cuba where the government there would be pleased to take care of the pirates.

The Pirate King had two pistols with mother-of-pearl handles, which Captain Alfie took off him as a souvenir, and a gold and silver brooch as his badge of office.

\*

Alfie awoke and dreamily reached under his pillow. He felt around until he found what he was looking for - the gold and silver brooch of the Pirate King. He smiled to himself and after wrapping the broach in tissue paper he put it with the coin and sword. What a wonderful bed – he could hardly wait to get back in it tonight.

# Chapter Four: The rate of exchange

Alfie sat reading his comic that came with the Sunday papers. He liked the cartoons and the wordsearch puzzles and today's were particularly tricky. He sat all afternoon in the garden after a big lunch of roast beef and Yorkshire pudding. His dog, Eddie, sat flaked out on the lawn beside him. He too liked a Sunday roast and helping to clear up any leftovers - he even liked vegetables (as long as they had gravy on them!).

Alfie's dad appeared with a football; he and Alfie took it in turns to keep goal at the end of the garden, whist his mum took her opportunity to read the papers and have a cup of tea. Eddie like to get involved too, he ran all round the garden pushing the football with his nose and keeping dad from getting it.

After tea and cakes the sun went in and they went indoors and watched television. All too soon it was bedtime and Alfie was nodding off in no time at all. Alfie loved the steady routine of Sundays, and normally was disappointed when it was bedtime. But tonight he didn't mind quite so much as he wondered if he would have another adventure onboard *The Labrador.*

*

The ship's timbers creaked as they sailed towards Cuba and the ship gently rolled from side to side in the gentle sea swell. Captain Alfie had just ensured that his pirate prisoners were well locked up and was now checking the charts to plot the final passage to Santiago de Cuba.

They were about three leagues away from the port, when the lookout reported smoke from the town. As they got closer they could see that the port was in ruins and was full of ships which had been sunk at their moorings. Some were still smoking above the waterline and masts were at crazy angles where they had been shot and broken by cannon balls. Captain Alfie and his ship had arrived after what had been a great battle.

After carefully mooring just outside the harbour Captain Alfie was rowed ashore in a longboat. He found the Governor in the remains of his mansion on the hill above the port. The Governor was in a bit of a state, and extremely pleased to see Captain Alfie. He explained that two nights ago four pirate ships had sneaked up in the dark and sunk or disabled every ship in the harbour with mighty broadsides from their cannons. They had surprised the troops on guard by attacking them from the land side with a small force and drawing them away from the port so that their shore cannons could be spiked and the ships could attack.

The attack was all over in two hours and the pirates had taken everything worth taking back to their ships. They searched the Governor's mansion for his money and they were mad when they couldn't find any.

So in order that the pirates could get him to hand his money over, they had kidnapped his daughter, Lady Grace, together with some other prominent citizens. The pirates were asking for a ransom of eighty thousand gold coins for their safe return!

The Governor was heartbroken at the loss of his beautiful daughter, Lady Grace, and the other valuable townspeople that the pirates had seized. He didn't have all that money and he couldn't see how to raise such a sum. He couldn't see a solution at all.

Captain Alfie told him not to worry and that he would try to come up with a plan.

The Pirate King was put into what was left of the jail with his men and Captain Alfie set to work planning.

The Governor told him that the pirates had instructed him to have a fire lit on Beacon Hill when he was ready to exchange the ransom for the kidnapped people. They would send a man with a message detailing the exchange position.

Captain Alfie suggested that to get the people and Lady Grace back they should try to exchange the Pirate King and some money for the prisoners, but to release the Pirate King needed the Governor's permission.

The fire was lit on Beacon Hill and a pirate appeared to take the proposals back to the rest of the pirates. Next day a message arrived that they would do an exchange for the Pirate King and twenty thousand gold pieces.

The townspeople gave all the money they could raise – floorboards were lifted and hidden purses were given to the Governor for the ransom but it was still several thousand coins short. Captain Alfie gathered his men on deck and explained to them about the shortage of coins. They all agreed that they would make up the difference with some of Captain Morgan's treasure that they had left.

It was dawn when *The Labrador* sailed from Santiago de Cuba with the Pirate King and twenty thousand coins on board. They were ordered to sail due east until they saw the pirate ship. They were then to heave to and stop. They sailed for two hours when the sailor in the crow's-nest reported that the pirates were in sight. *The Labrador's* sails were lowered and she slowed to a stop in the calm seas.

The pirates sailed to within a distance just outside cannon range and lowered a boat with the prisoners in it. *The Labrador's* crew also lowered a longboat and placed the ransom and the Pirate King in it. The two longboats rowed to within shouting distance of each other and Captain Alfie could see the pirate's captain with his black patch on one eye and a hook where his left hand should have been. He could also see the Lady Grace who was the most beautiful girl he had ever seen. He knew that he must save her and her companions from this evil looking man.

With pistols pointing at each other the two captains changed boats with each other and then their men who had been rowing also changed over. The two boats then rowed back to their ships, each captain closely watching the other. It was rare for a ransom to go wrong, as it was how most pirates got by and it was probably the only thing that they did with any honour.

However, once the exchange was completed it was back to normal and the enemies could attack each other. Expecting an attack, Captain Alfie had readied his crew to leave and had ordered his cannons to be lowered, ready to fire if they were fired upon. He didn't really want to fight as he had the Lady Grace and kidnapped citizens on board. As a precaution that they couldn't be trusted, he had ordered that a cannon be mounted in his captain's quarters in the stern of the ship facing the rear.

The pirates were true to their bad form and they lined up to chase and attack *The Labrador*. Captain Alfie put on as much sail as the ship could take but in the light wind the pirates were gaining on them. They had a big surprise when the windows of the captain's cabin were opened up and a heavy cannon ball came hurtling in their direction. They turned away and broke off their attack – they had got the Pirate King back and twenty thousand gold coins. They had done well! No need to be too greedy!

Once back in port, there were huge cheers and celebrations. The Lady Grace was so pleased to see her father that she gave Captain Alfie a big kiss for saving her, in front of *everyone*. The crew all went "Woooooooooo!" and Captain Alfie went bright red.

The Governor made Captain Alfie stand to attention and he awarded him a large medal for his bravery and then asked him to take tea with him and the Lady Grace.

*

"Cup of tea Alfie?" his mother said as she gently woke him up.

# Chapter Five: The medal

Alfie reached out and took the teacup carefully from his mother and drank it like he was in a drinking contest. "Careful," said his mother, "It's not a race you know!"

But it was, as Alfie wanted to know if he still had his medal of bravery, and he couldn't check whilst his mum was still in the room. After she left, taking the cup with her, Alfie rolled over in bed and reached under the pillow. He could feel nothing; he lifted up the pillow and looked, but the medal was nowhere to be seen. Alfie thought that perhaps the bed had lost its powers and that that was the end of it all. He was downcast as he ate his cornflakes and toast.

His dad noticed and asked if there was anything wrong. "A penny for them?" he said.

Alfie brightened and laughed, "These days it will cost you a pound! Times have moved on from Granddad's day you know, that's just the sort of thing Granddad always says!" said Alfie, and his dad laughed. "But I think I may have lost something, Dad." Alfie added.

As usual, parents sometimes have some good advice. His dad said, "Well, remember where you had it last and start looking from there."

Alfie thought about this all day at school and in Geography he took out his atlas book and looked up a place called Cuba and much to his astonishment it existed, as did a place called Santiago. If that's where I saw the medal last, how ever can

I get it back, he wondered? As he looked at the map he began to remember the Governor pinning the medal on his chest and try as he might he could remember no more.

Alfie's mum had gone shopping, so Alfie walked back to Grace's house with Grace and her mother, and was having tea there today. He decided to tell Grace all about his adventures as he was bursting to tell someone and she was alright for a girl. She thought that the adventures sounded great and she particularly liked the thought of a Lady Grace being in the story. "She sounds a bit like she has never heard of girl power," said Grace. "If it were my story, it would be the ladies who save the day. So you got a medal did you, my hero, and now you've lost it."

Girls are masters of the obvious, thought Alfie.

"Perhaps you put it into your tunic pocket for safe keeping," she suggested.

That's it! thought Alfie. It's in my pyjama top pocket.

Alfie's mum collected him and took him home. Alfie opened the gate like a proper little gentleman and helped his mum carry the shopping in from the car. As his mum put the shopping away he went upstairs to his room to see if the medal was in his pyjama top. To his horror, his pyjamas had gone. His mother had washed them and, by the noise from the utility room, they were in the spin dryer. Alfie stood by the dryer until the programme had finished and he reached in and pulled out the red hot pyjamas.

"Keen to get to bed?" his mum said teasingly. Alfie said he was trying to help out as he felt in the top pocket of the pyjamas but to no avail.

Where was that medal? He went back to his bed and looked under the pillow and then in a flash of inspiration he pulled the bed away from the wall. There it was – it had fallen down the back of the bed! Alfie picked it up and studied it carefully under the lamp beside his bed. It was big and round and engraved with the words To A Hero, it was hung

from a big red ribbon with a safety pin.

Alfie tried it on and looked in the mirror. As he did so his appearance changed and he had a big captain's hat and military tunic on. The captain's sword and jewelled badge of the Pirate King sparkled back at him. Alfie turned to one side to look at himself and the image went back to being him in his school blazer with the medal pinned on the front.

Eddie came in from his walk with dad to greet him and lay down on Alfie's bed with his legs in the air to let Alfie tickle him. Eddie loved his little master and licked him as hard and as often as he could to prove it.

Alfie put the medal in his drawer with his other treasures and started getting ready to go to bed. At this rate I'll be able to fill a chest, he thought!

Alfie pulled the duvet cover over his shoulders and sank into the wonderful softness of the bed, it was calling him again, it was saying "Rest your tired little head, Alfie, you've had a busy, busy day." Alfie willingly drifted off to sleep.

# Chapter Six: Come in sir

Captain Alfie shivered as he pulled his overcoat tighter to try to keep out the cold winds that wanted to cut him in half. Though he had missed England and his home, he didn't miss the winter cold. The Caribbean seemed a million miles away and yet it had been only three weeks ago that *The Labrador* had been sailing the warm, deep blue seas.

His navigation had been spot on and the crew all lined the decks as they sailed slowly past Land's End in the cold light of dawn. They were pleased to be home and they knew that they would be in Portsmouth before the day was out.

The decks were alive that day as sails were tidied and decks scrubbed. Captain Alfie was looking forward to docking *The Labrador,* seeing his home port and reporting to his Admiral before some well-earned shore leave. The seagulls shrieked as they glided in and out of the ships' masts; they were looking for scraps. The crew men amused themselves by throwing bits of food into the air for the gulls to dive and catch.

As Portsmouth came into sight, the sails were trimmed back and *The Labrador* slowed to a crawl as Captain Alfie commanded the helmsman to steer one way and then the other until the ship docked. The crew were all in their finest uniforms to meet their wives and relatives who were waving and cheering as *The Labrador* docked. The gangplank was lowered and the bosun blew his whistle as a salute for the Admiral who came on board.

As the men were all leaving the ship to visit home, Captain Alfie undertook to tell the Admiral of his voyage. Captain Alfie had wanted to visit home too but he was in charge and he had to finish his duties first. The Admiral had heard all about Captain Alfie's adventures and told him that he was to be promoted! The King had asked for him to visit London where he was to be honoured for his bravery and for the great treasures he had brought back with him for the King.

Captain Alfie packed his chest of clothes and supervised the treasure barrels being loaded into a big coach which the Admiral had organised to take him to see the King.

The coachmen shook the reins of the four horses pulling the coach and they were off. The coach lumbered slowly and bumpily along the dirt and gravel road. Captain Alfie made himself as comfortable as he could and sat back to look at the countryside as they passed it slowly by.

The coach had an escort of four armed men on horses who rode two in front and two at the rear. The treasure on board the coach was a magnet for thieves and vagabonds and needed protection for its trip to the King.

The trip to London would take about three days and the first day passed without incident; the coach drew into the yard of an inn called the Foresters Arms. The landlord showed Captain Alfie to his room for the night before bringing him food and drink, and throwing another log on the roaring fire. Nothing is too much trouble for a hero! Captain Alfie could hear the noise of the horses being stabled and the soldiers mounting a guard on the treasure. The soldiers took it in turns to be on guard duty all night in two hour shifts.

The coach drivers were awake at five o'clock, grooming and feeding the horses. Breakfast was served and the coach pulled away from the inn. As they were leaving, Captain Alfie noticed a man lurking in the shadows at the side of the stables who promptly vanished into the woods at the side of the inn. Captain Alfie decided to take a few precautions.

The road narrowed as it approached a thickly wooded area and, even though the sun was shining brightly, the light had a job to break through the dense foliage. Captain Alfie decided to ride up with the coachmen with his pistol loaded and ready for any trouble. If anybody wanted trouble he was just the person to give it to them - after all he had fought the roughest pirates in the world to get it and he was determined to keep it!

"Look out," shouted the coachman as he saw two men drop onto two soldiers in front from a big branch that crossed the road. The two guards fell from their horses and were overpowered, as were the two guards behind.

Captain Alfie stood up and fired his pistol, which was signal for the guards to snap into action. From inside the coach, four guards and a large bull mastiff dog (which he had borrowed from the Inn's landlord) jumped out and a fierce hand-to-hand fight began. The attackers suddenly decided that there were too many guards and ran away, disappearing into the thick woods empty-handed.

"Well done, men," said Captain Alfie. "That's seen them off. Let's get going."

Captain Alfie was glad that, after seeing a suspicious man in the shadows at the Foresters Arms, he had put a plan into action. He had got four of the stable hands to ride the guards' horses and put the proper guards inside the coach, so if they were attacked then they could surprise the robbers – and they had. He laughed as he thought of the robbers running away, with one of them having lost the seat of his trousers to the dog which stood watching them flee with the piece of red trouser cloth in its mouth.

After about and hour the road widened and turned to open countryside. The danger passed, the stable hands were paid and sent back with the dog to the inn. The coach carried on its way and soon the outskirts of London were reached.

The King had sent an escort for the last few miles and Captain Alfie was soon ushered into the palace by a very grand man who said he was the King's assistant. The palace was impressive with its high ceilings, ornate edgings and gilt decor; flags and coats of arms were hanging from every wall. Then they came to a large set of high double doors with a guard on duty at either side. The doors opened and Captain Alfie was ushered in. The King of England sat on a throne, on a raised area at one end of the hall; he was surrounded by courtiers and ministers.

"Ah, Captain Alfie, come in," said the King. "I have been told about your exploits and the nation is grateful to you for the bravery you have shown and the treasure you have brought us. I have decided to award you a knighthood." said the King genially. "You may approach, and kneel."

Captain Alfie kneeled and the King waved a sword over his head and touched him lightly on each shoulder. "Arise, Sir Alfred, Knight of the Realm." The king then gave Sir Alfred a velvet sash and jewel of office.

*

"Rise and shine, the night's over," his mother said as she gently shook Alfie by the shoulders to wake him up.

# Chapter Seven: The Incan Puzzle

Alfie was soon out of bed, washed and dressed and feeling under his pillow.

He carefully folded up the velvet sash and, with the jewel of a knight that he found under his pillow, he placed the items into his drawer.

In two minutes he was sat down at the breakfast table eating his sausage, egg and bacon with hot buttered toast. Eddie loved it when Alfie had a cooked breakfast as he could usually beg at least a half sausage and a piece of crispy bacon off his young master. "Don't keep feeding him food," said Alfie's mother, "He's too fat already."

But Eddie had already run out of the back door, with half a sausage delicately held between his teeth as it was far too hot to gobble up immediately.

At school, Alfie's teacher asked him to read out loud to the rest of the class from a big story book. She helped him with the long words and soon it was someone else's turn. Alfie took his seat and stared out of the window, glad that today was a half day and that his dad was picking him up to go to a rugby match.

The school bell rang for the end of morning classes and Alfie was first into the cloakroom to put on his coat and first to stand by the school gate to look for his dad.

The teacher on the gate kept all the pupils in until their parents picked them up. Where was Alfie's dad? Alfie paced up and down and it was not long before the playground was nearly empty.

Alfie's dad pulled up in his car and Alfie was let out of the playground by the teacher who was pleased to get off home and have a well earned cup of tea and lunch.

"Where have you been?" said Alfie.

"Sorry, Alfie, my boss wanted me to finish some paperwork before I finished for the day," said his dad. "Still, I've got enough time to go to the match now."

After a quick lunch Alfie's mother wrapped her little gentleman in a scarf and anorak, she kissed him on the cheek (leaving a big red mark on his face from her lipstick!) and he left for the rugby match.

Alfie liked going to the matches with his dad who loved rugby. Alfie didn't understand all the rules but he enjoyed watching the sides compete for the ball and to see the backs running and passing the ball. He marvelled at the kicks for goal over the posts and he decided that he wanted to be a kicker when he grew up. He loved the atmosphere as the kicker lined up to take the kick, the silence as he took the kick and then the jubilation in one half of the crowd as the ball sailed over - or the groan of disappointment if the ball missed.

Alfie's home team had the ball and a winger swept past his opposite man after a long pass and scored on the try line. The crowd was so loud in its applause that Alfie put his hands over his ears.

His dad said, "That's what you need to win in this game – good tactics."

The referee blew his whistle and the game was over, the crowd left the ground and Alfie and his dad left with them; they were soon home.

Alfie told his mum all about the match as he ate his tea. "That's nice, dear," she said as she busied herself around the kitchen. Alfie thought, she always says that.

Alfie watched television with Eddie at his side who woofed occasionally when he saw a cat on an advert. He sometimes ran and looked round the back of the TV to see if the cat had hidden there. The time for bed drew near and Alfie's dad went upstairs with him to make sure he brushed his teeth properly before going to bed.

Alfie yawned as he sank into the deep soft sheets on his bed. They were fresh on today and they smelled of flowers.

*

A bright green parrot shrieked at the top of its voice and flew past Alfie, the jungle explorer's head. His sea-captain's uniform had now been replaced by the khaki coloured clothes of the jungle. The parrot nearly knocked the floppy hat off his head. Alfie stopped to consult his map and check his course with a small pocket compass. The jungle in South America was hot and steaming and he took a swig of water from his water bottle. Alfie looked back and saw that the row of porters carrying the camping gear, food and water had stopped to take a break as well. As it would soon be dark they set up camp and, by the light of a candle, Alfie the explorer studied the map to the lost city of the Incas called Machu Picchu. He saw a pyramid marked on the map and on the side was written in Incan, "Puzzle pyramid."

He hoped that they would soon find proof that the map was genuine and not a big joke that someone had played on him at the Royal Explorer's Club.

Alfie sat by the fire and listened to the sound of the jungle at night. He could hear the insects buzzing and the animals calling to each other in the dark. The heat had died down a bit but it started to rain in buckets and stair rods, as his granddad used to say. Alfie realised now why it was called a rainforest. He retired to his camp bed and tied up the mosquito net tightly.

The next morning the jungle floor was steaming as the native porters packed up and they set off.

They had been going for an hour up a very steep slope when Alfie's jungle machete hit something hard as he slashed at the thick jungle creepers in front of him. It was an Inca statue that had been hidden by the thick green jungle for years. Alfie hacked away the growth until he could see the statue was that of a fierce warrior god with bright red ruby eyes. The native porters took one look at it and they backed away and hid in the jungle; they were superstitious and easily frightened. It took all of Alfie's powers of persuasion to get them to come back.

They pressed on, up and up the slope until they were standing at the bottom of a huge pyramid. It was made of stone with steps on the front that went up and up, through the low cloud, to the top. Alfie whooped with joy at the find. The map was true and he had found Machu Picchu, the lost city of the Incas.

Alfie climbed up the long set of steps and when he got to the top he was puffed. He sat down to get his breath back on a flat table-type stone, marvelling at the vista spread out before him. He was so high up he could see the tops of trees in the jungle below him; trees that had towered so high above him just a couple of days ago. In the distance, Alfie could see layers of mountains through the thinning cloud.

Soon he stood up and started looking around the top of the pyramid. He noticed that the statues of the various gods that the Incas worshipped were arranged like they were pieces on a giant chess board. There were two of each one, either in black or white and about three feet tall. Two full sets, thought Alfie, I wonder what tactics you need to win this game.

The top of the pyramid was covered in symbols engraved in the floor and Alfie tried to see if he could work out what they meant. He looked at them without having a clue for a while.

He was about to go back down when he accidentally bumped into a statue and he just caught it from falling over. But it was quite heavy and he had to lower it to the floor. As he did so he noticed that there was an engraved symbol on the bottom of the statue that matched one on the floor. All the others were the same and each had a different symbol on its bottom.

Alfie the explorer got his native porters to place the statues one by one on the top of the symbols they matched. Just as the last statue was being placed on the correct spot, the floor of the pyramid started to move in the centre and began to sink down.

All the porters ran down the steps screaming that the world was about to end, but Alfie the explorer stood firm and gazed down the neat square hole that appeared.

He could see a golden door on one side of the hole. He leaped in and forced the golden door open with his jungle machete. Just inside he found a big mirror of polished metal and what could only be described as a tripod stand.

He had noticed three holes in the floor at the top of the square hole. The tripod fitted them exactly and the polished golden mirror of metal rested on it. The sun caught the mirror and a shaft of bright light lit the chamber behind the golden door.

Alfie couldn't believe his eyes; the chamber was full of big clay pots, filled with gold and silver nugget pieces which sparkled in the beam of light. He had found a long lost city and a long lost treasure.

Alfie the explorer got his men to collect the pots and take them down to the bottom of the pyramid. He picked up two pieces of gold and one of silver that had been dropped by the porters as he followed them down the steps and put them in his pocket.

Alfie was almost at the bottom when he slipped on the

steps and sat down on his bottom with a thump and the sound of his compass glass breaking.

*

Alfie went to get up and he realised that he had just fallen out of bed and had knocked over a water glass by his bed. He struggled between sleep and wakefulness as his mum rushed in, woken by the noise. She cleared up the glass and settled Alfie back to sleep as it was still the middle of the night. Alfie was soon nodding off again but before he did, he felt under his pillow. He found what he was looking for - one silver and two gold nuggets. More for his collection, Alfie thought, slipping out of bed to put them in his drawer before settling back down to continue his night-time adventures.

*

Alfie the explorer reached into his back pocket to find that he had broken his compass when he slipped. This was a disaster! How would he ever find his way out of the thick jungle without a compass to check his bearings?

Alfie got the native porters to cook dinner whilst he sat to consider his position. He consulted his head porter who thought he could perhaps find their way out of the jungle if they followed their way in. This sounded simple but could be quite difficult as the daily rains wiped out all trace of their tracks in the jungle from the days before.

No, Alfie the explorer needed a better plan to be sure of getting back out.

Alfie looked at the compass and the pin, which the needle spun on, was broken and there was no hope of mending it. Alfie was thinking how he could use the compass needle and get it to point to magnetic North. He pulled a cork from a bottle to have a drink and he accidentally dropped the cork into a tin mug half full of water.

Eureka! thought Alfie the explorer. The cork was floating on the water. Alfie took the magnetic compass needle and rested it on a slice of floating cork. The needle swung to point to magnetic North. "It works!" shouted Alfie, and next day he started to lead the expedition out of the jungle holding a tin mug as a compass.

He was just walking under a tree eating a jungle banana when a monkey jumped down on him and stole the fruit and he tipped some of the water from the mug on his face.

*

Alfie woke up with Eddie licking his face and lying on top of him. He felt something hard under his neck and discovered the tin mug, compass needle and piece of cork.

# Chapter Eight: A Treasured reflection

Alfie brushed his shoes for school, thinking about the jungle and the Inca treasure and he wondered how Alfie the explorer would get out in one piece.

At school that day Alfie asked his teacher about the Incas and the teacher found him a book all about them.

Alfie read that they were a fierce warrior race and they existed between 1200 and 1535AD. They built big temples, paved roads and irrigation systems on the steep slopes of the Andes. They worshipped a sun god called Inti and an earth god called Pachamama; they were good farmers who paid their taxes in gold.

They were wiped out by 180 Spanish Conquistadors who were commanded by Francisco Pizzaro. The Incas were no match for the Spanish guns. The Spaniards took their gold and sent it back to Spain. It was fascinating stuff.

After lunch of Shepherd's Pie and Alfie's favourite sweet, chocolate splodge with custard, it was time for another lesson.

Alfie spent all afternoon painting a picture of the Inca Pyramid and the thick green jungle that surrounded it. He filled the paper with parrots, monkeys and a big snake that coiled around a branch on a tree. When he had finished, the teacher was so impressed she gave Alfie a gold star and hung his picture on the classroom wall.

Alfie was pleased to get to bed that night. He had worked hard all day at school, and had been for a long walk with his dad and Eddie in the park. Eddie was tired as well through chasing the ball, he stretched out beside Alfie's bed and soon the two of them were snoring.

*

Alfie the explorer sat up and straightened his hat as the monkey ran away with his jungle banana. He put his makeshift compass back together and sat checking the map. He noticed that the map showed a stone statue like a big bird on the side of a nearby mountain. It looked like it may be a short cut back to civilization.

He set off to look, as it was not too far out of their way. They had been looking for the statue for an hour when they came to a narrow ravine. It was just too far to jump over and too deep to climb down and up the other side. They followed the ravine along its side and they found a flat path that wound alongside the ravine.

The walking was easy now and Alfie the explorer hoped that it was a secret path built by the Incas to cross the mountain. Around a corner they suddenly saw a giant statue of a condor (the big bird of the Andes). The condor stood with its head stretched out towards the mountain and its wings were a bridge across the ravine.

The native porters were very careful as they crossed the bridge; they insisted that Alfie went first to check it was alright and safe. They decided to stop for a rest as the high altitude made them strain to get their breath.

The flat stone path seemed to disappear into the rock face of the mountain. They chopped a few creepers down and found the entrance to a cave hidden by the foliage.

Inside the cave entrance they found another statue and it had engraved beneath it that it was the earth god Pachamama. All the native porters knelt down and gave thanks to the earth god and left him flowers to bless their journey through the cave. They lit torches and followed Alfie the explorer down into the dark depths of the mountain. They went down and down, deeper and deeper into the mountain. Giant bats flew out as they were disturbed by the men, flying past within inches but missing everyone.

Alfie was in front when he noticed a reflection from something off to the side. It was another cave and it was full of old Spanish armour and muskets. They were from the Spanish Conquistadors; perhaps even Francisco Pizzaro had come this way with his looted Incan gold, thought Alfie.

The porters managed to carry some of the armour and they pressed on. Alfie the explorer could see a faint white light in the distance; this light got brighter as they got nearer and soon they emerged from the bottom of the mountain, stepping out into brilliant sunlight.

They had inadvertently found a quick way back to civilization and before long they were in the town of Cuzco. From here they could hire a boat and follow the river all the way down to Lake Titicaca before commencing an arduous trek back to La Paz in Bolivia. This took many days, but once he arrived in La Paz, Alfie the explorer could catch a train with the treasure. He was taking it back to the British Museum where he could tell his tale at a lecture to the Royal Explorer's Society.

The steam train whistle blew and the carriage that Alfie the explorer sat in jolted as the engine pulled away from the station.

*

Alfie woke up with a jolt too; he looked under his pillow and found a Spanish gunpowder horn with the name of its owner engraved on it – FRANCISCO PIZZARO.

# Chapter Nine: Lead in the Air

It was one of those "great to be alive" days. The sun was shining and the horse chestnut trees were covered in large spiney-cased conkers. Alfie's dad took him and Eddie down to the park to play. All Eddie wanted to do was run around like a mad thing and roll on his back in the grass. Alfie got his dad to reach up into the tree and get him some conkers down. He was determined to find the biggest, brownest and hardest conker he could find. He suddenly saw a huge conker and was about to pick it up when Eddie dashed up, picked up the conker and ran away with it.

"Come back here, you," Alfie called after him as he chased him around the grass and in between the trees. Eddie loved a good chase and he was an expert at dodging his young master. After a while he was puffed out and he sat down and dropped the conker at Alfie's feet. Alfie picked it up, wiping Eddie's saliva off it before putting it into his pocket with a dozen others. His dad then decided it was time to go home, but he said he would help Alfie make his battling conkers.

Alfie went into the garage watched as his dad took a drill and bored small neat holes through all of Alfie's conkers. He then took a ball of string from a shelf and cut some two feet lengths of string and passed each through the hole in each conker. He tied each one with a double knot. "There," he said, "Let's get a knock-out session started. Go and get Mum."

They then spent the next hour trying to teach Alfie how to hold the string and then how to strike his opponent's conker to knock it off its string and win. Alfie's dad gave him lots of helpful advice and soon Alfie was playing like a champion.

Alfie polished the large brown conker until it shone like it was covered in glass.

That's perfect, he thought as he put it beside his bed; he was determined to beat all comers in the school playground championships that were to be held next day at school.

Alfie lay in bed that night and before long the plumped-up duvet had turned into great white clouds that floated past the windows of the narrow gauge railway that Alfie the explorer was on. The railway wound on up the steep slopes and it was over fifteen thousand feet high before it began to descend from the snow-covered mountains of the Andes down towards Buenos Aires which was over a thousand miles away at sea level. The mountains were a desolate bare landscape and very little employment was available except mining (which was dangerous) and banditry, particularly train robbing. This was why each train had a small force of military guards on it.

Alfie the explorer had checked that the Inca treasure and the Spanish armour was safely locked up in the steel guard's van before he went to the small dining car for some food and coffee. He had just finished eating when there was a loud explosion from in front of the steam engine. The brakes squealed as the driver pulled a lever as hard as he could. The plates and cups went flying all around Alfie as he clung to the seat and table where he sat. Then gunfire broke out all round him as the train was shot at by bandits hidden in the rocks near the front of the train. The windows were soon full of neat round bullet holes as Alfie the explorer took cover under the table. The train's guards were soon firing back and the bandits got a big surprise that there were so many of them. This was because Alfie and his treasure was an important cargo and the railway supervisor had doubled the guard in its honour.

The bandits soon decided that perhaps it was not the easiest of trains to rob. They melted back into the mountains to escape from the guards who were much better armed; the guards chased the bandits and when they were satisfied that the danger was passed they came back to the train.

The engineer stood scratching his head as he looked at the track in front of the engine. The bandits had blown up the track and a piece of the rail was all bent, buckled and broken. The train could not go on, it would have to reverse all the way back to the last station (ten hours back!).

Alfie the explorer heard what the engineer had said and he thought about their problem. He then suggested to the driver and engineer that they could perhaps mend the track so they could go on. "How?" they asked together. They had the tools and plenty of guards to help but no spare rails.

Alfie said, "Why not take up a rail from behind the train and lay it in front to replace the damaged section."

"Brilliant," said the engineer and he set about organising the men to change the rail. With much huffing and puffing an hour later the track was repaired. Alfie picked up a spare nut and bolt from the track and put it in his bag as a memento of his brush with the bandits. The train carried on to the next station where they sent a telegram to the railway supervisor so that he could send a repair crew to mend the missing rail.

The train took over two more days to reach the flat open pampas of Argentina, and Alfie the explorer was pleased to see the land getting flatter and greener as they neared Buenos Aires. The pampas was full of grazing beef cattle with the Argentinean cowboys (called gauchos) rounding them up to move them on to fresh grass. The train stopped to fill up with water and Alfie got out, stretching his legs. He saw two gauchos chase a steer that was determined to get away; they were twirling bolas around their head and when they let go the three balls on string wrapped themselves around the steer's legs, making the steer fall over. The gauchos soon put a rope

on it and led it away with the rest of the herd. The train blew its whistle and set off again for Buenos Aires.

Alfie the explorer wondered if it would really be "good air" in Buenos Aires as the English translation of the name meant.

The style of houses and public buildings got grander and grander as the train neared the city. The small huts gave way to buildings covered in fancy stonework and huge entrances, with wide streets and elegant gardens. The train finally pulled to a stop at the main central station.

Alfie the explorer and his cargo were taken to the Grande Hotel where Alfie had a well earned hot bath. Later after lunch he went to see a shipping agent to find out when the next ship would leave for England. The agent sat in his dockside office puffing a big cigar that made Alfie the explorer's eyes water.

"You're in luck, Senor, there is a ship leaving tomorrow for Gibraltar, you will pick up another ship there."

The next day, after a comfortable night in the Grande Hotel, Alfie the explorer stood on the deck of the ship as the thick mooring ropes were lifted from the dockside bollards and the ship blew its whistle and set out to sea. The funnel was belching thick smoke as the water churned and boiled, and the propeller strained to push the steel ship forward.

Alfie the explorer always liked setting out to sea and as he stood on deck he noticed that the water around the estuary entrance was full of seals dancing in the waves. He stood and watched them, mesmerized until the sun had set. Alfie ambled back to his cabin, and settled down to write up his diary and work out his lecture to The Royal Explorers Society. After dinner he took a walk around the deck before returning to his cabin and, after a couple of attempts, he managed to climb into his hammock. The deep steady drum of the engines on the ship was like a heartbeat and Alfie the explorer soon nodded off.

# Chapter Ten: Monkee business

Alfie woke up to the gentle buzzing of his new multi-tone alarm clock. As was becoming his habit every morning now, he reached quickly under his pillow and found his new treasure - a large steel railway nut and bolt. He wrapped it in tissue paper and put it in the drawer amongst the other treasures from his night time adventures.

Eddie was already up and sitting by the back door, asking to be let out. Alfie let him out before sitting at the table and pouring out a huge bowl of cornflakes. These adventures really give me an appetite, he thought.

He picked up his conkers and set off for school. Today was the day that he was going to put all of his dad's training to good use and beat his class mates at conkers.

The championship began at break and carried on at lunchtime. As the afternoon bell was rung the contestants had been whittled down to just four. Alfie was still amongst them with his big conker, which was a five times winner already.

The afternoon classes finished and the contestants began knocking away at each other. Soon Alfie was in the final against William, who for the day was calling himself William the Conqueror! They tossed a coin to see who started first and Alfie lost. He had to hold his conker still when William lined up an enormous blow and bashed Alfie's conker. Alfie's conker split in two and fell to the ground. He had lost to William the

Conqueror. He felt the stab of disappointment just for a moment but then he told himself that he was second and that's not bad!

Alfie reached into his pocket and pulled out the strings of conkers that his dad had made for him. He had tied them all together at one end so that the strings wouldn't tangle. "Best of three tomorrow!" he called to William who had run round the playground on a lap of honour. "OK," William called back.

Alfie's Mum appeared by the gate and Alfie went to meet her. They were walking home down the High Street with Alfie telling his mum how he was so close to nearly winning, when a youth ran by and snatched his mother's handbag. Alfie's mum yelped in surprise, then started shouting whilst Alfie stood helplessly by.

The youth was running away with the bag when Alfie had a brainwave. He felt in his pocket for his conkers, thinking of how the gauchos swung their bolas. He twirled them round his head and let them fly at the running youth's legs. Other people had seen what had happened and were chasing the youth, when suddenly he came crashing down onto the pavement - with the conker strings and conkers wrapped in a tangle around his legs. A man jumped on top of the youth and held him until the police arrived. His mum got her handbag back, then she and Alfie had to see a nice police lady who took his mother's statement so that the youth could be dealt with in court.

The police lady thought Alfie was very clever throwing the conkers and their strings at the running youth. She asked where he had got the idea from.

"Oh, a gaucho gave me the idea!" Alfie said, then added with a cheeky laugh, "…perhaps the chief constable should issue you all with bolas."

Alfie's mother was so proud of him when she told his dad all about it. "He's mummy's little hero." She always says that, thought Alfie. Eddie just went "Humph!" as he wanted to be the centre of attention. If he'd been there, he'd have chased the thief and dog-tackled him.

"Come on, even superheroes have to go to bed," said his dad as he took Alfie up to bed. Alfie was still telling his dad how he nearly beat William as he tucked him in. But tomorrow would be better.

*

The pace of life on the ship was slow and the constant whirl and hum of the ship's engines seemed to penetrate every part of the deck and cabins as Alfie the explorer tried to find a quiet place to read a magazine that he had picked up in Buenos Aires.

Last night he had had dinner with the captain and crew. They had had roast beef and Yorkshire pudding followed by trifle. Alfie had missed the comforts of home and on this British owned ship he felt quite at home. The captain (a man with a big ginger beard and weather-beaten face) had explained that they were going to travel through Iceberg Alley where there was a danger from icebergs. He had doubled the lookout and expected no trouble, but all passengers and crew would have to have an emergency drill.

The icebergs were giant lumps of ice that had broken away from the Antarctic and they drifted slowly northwards with the currents, so they were a danger to shipping.

He warned that the bit that you could see above water was only about one tenth of what was below the waterline.

Later that day, after a lifeboat drill, the captain called the passengers together to show them an iceberg that the lookouts had warned him about. The ship altered course slightly to pass safely by and Alfie looked at the iceberg which seemed to be a beautiful blue and brilliant white. The captain explained that the blueness was as a result of the sunlight being deflected by the ice crystals and split up like a prism into its basic colours. The big icebergs were usually avoided easily but he warned that it was smaller icebergs called "growlers" that lay just on or below the surface that were a danger. He said that as they were obviously in Iceberg Alley now he would slow the ship down.

That evening Alfie the explorer was walking on the deck when the ship shuddered slightly and a grinding noise was heard. The ship's alarm whistle went and everyone was called to lifeboat stations. The ship had struck a growler and the captain ordered his crew to check for damage whilst the passengers were to put on lifejackets, just in case.

The first mate reported to the captain that the damage was not much but a small split in the hull which was leaking slightly. The bilge pumps were turned up to full and they appeared to be coping well.

Alfie the explorer offered to help the crew and he was put to work to stem the leak.

The chief engineer with Alfie and the crew folded up a canvas sheet and pressed it to the leaking split with a series of wooden props which were hammered into place to keep the canvas tight up against the hull. This worked well and the danger passed.

The ship was soon back up to full speed and heading for Gibraltar where it could go into dry dock and be repaired.

A week's sailing later and Alfie the explorer could see the giant Rock of Gibraltar looming over the Straits between Europe and the North African port of Tangier.

The ship was joined by dolphins swimming at the front of the ship's bows. They darted in and out of the water playing a game as if welcoming the ship into harbour.

The harbour at Gibraltar was a crossroads of the shipping world and ships of every nation were moored up with their countries' flags flying proudly from their sterns.

The captain gave Alfie the explorer a flag as thanks for

his help in the emergency and wished him well for his journey back to Britain.

Alfie the explorer was met on the dockside by a representative of the Governor who invited the famous explorer to stay with him in the Governor's Cottage. The Inca treasure was safely locked up in the Customs strong room and Alfie's taxi took him to the cottage to meet the Governor.

The cottage was a lot more impressive than its name suggested and it had one of the best views in Gibraltar. You could look north to see Spain, or southwards over the straits towards Tangier and the Moroccan coast with the Atlas Mountains in the distance.

The Governor listened with great interest to Alfie's adventures. and the Governor then offered to take Alfie on a tour of Gibralter, and tell him about its history.

Gibraltar was given to the British as spoils of war against the Spanish in the seventeenth century. There have been sieges by the Spanish which led to the numerous galleries carved out of the rock to house guns and defences. The Governor took Alfie to the fortifications and showed him the view from the very top of the rock.

The seaward side of The Rock was a sheer drop of fourteen hundred feet and Alfie the explorer marvelled at the Barbary Apes that had made their home there. They were without fear as they leaped from rock to rock. The Barbary Apes were fed every day by the British soldiers as they had done since the early seventeen hundreds. The legend says that if the Barbary Apes ever leave the Rock then so will the British.

The tour over with, Alfie the explorer started to work out his way back to Britain. He went to a shipping agent's office and found that he could wangle a trip home on a Royal Navy destroyer. The destroyer had huge guns and a crew of several hundred men.

The ship slipped its moorings in the Naval Dockyard and set sail into the night bound for Portsmouth. Alfie the explorer had a very comfortable cabin to himself and the captain had lent him a dinner jacket, as the ship's officers always dressed up for dinner. Alfie the explorer felt very grand in the dinner jacket and black bow tie as he sat down at the wonderfully laid out table with polished glasses, white linen napkins and polished silver cutlery.

All the officers stood out of respect as the captain entered the wardroom. Stewards with white jackets served them with dinner using ladles, spoons and forks to place the various courses onto the dinner plates from their silver serving flats. They had soup first, and then roast pork and stuffing followed by cream caramel. Alfie was full to bursting when they brought coffee. They then all stood up and toasted the health of the Queen, whose picture hung on the wall behind the captain.

The officers and captain were all keen to hear about Alfie the explorer's adventures and were pleased when he showed them some Inca gold and silver, as well as the Spanish helmet of the Conquistadors. They sat in the wardroom and passed the Port decanter around the table to the left, as was tradition.

Alfie the explorer was pleased to get back to his cabin that night as he felt very tired from the effects of the huge dinner he had eaten. The wind whistled around the porthole as the destroyer forged its way through the building seas.

# Chapter Eleven: Fishermen in the nets

The gust of wind was so strong that it blew Alfie's window wide open and a blast of air soon brought Alfie to his senses. He leapt out of bed and closed the rattling window tightly shut. Eddie had not moved a muscle; he was in his basket, on his back with his legs in the air. Alfie thought that Eddie was a master of the art of relaxation.

Alfie took out the ship's flag from under his pillow, carefully folded it up and stowed it in his drawer.

He washed his face and cleaned his teeth as he looked forward to a return bout with William the Conqueror at school. He took some of his dad's shaving foam and rubbed it on his face like he was going to shave. His dad laughed when he looked in the bathroom to see Alfie shaving his face with the back of a comb.

"You've got a few years yet before you need to shave, young man!" said his dad.

Alfie said that he could feel stubble on his chin and he needed to shave it off. His dad laughed.

Alfie was soon on his way to school with a fistful of conkers and a thirst for revenge.

Alfie and William were still playing conkers when the teacher told them to stop and come in for lessons. "Just when I was winning," said William.

Alfie smiled and said, "You wish!"

The two boys battled at lunchtime without a clear winner and in class that afternoon they were playfully taunting each other. The teacher told them off for talking and told them to behave or she would send them to the headmaster's office. They both behaved until school finished and then they were back out in the playground for round three of the duel.

Both boys' conkers were looking a little the worse for wear when Alfie caught William's conker a fatal blow. The conkers flew in all directions and Alfie became Alfie the Conqueror. His celebrations were shortlived, as another classmate called Lucy stepped up with a challenge.

Alfie could not be shown up by refusing a conker fight with a girl, so he accepted her challenge with a polite shrug. Alfie agreed to 'let ladies go first' but he was shocked when she pulled from her pocket the biggest conker he had ever seen. It was like a hammer as it hit his conker and shattered it.

"Beaten by a girl! Beaten by a girl!" chanted William who was suddenly feeling better after seeing Alfie taken down a peg or two.

Alfie congratulated Lucy on beating him and then asked her which tree she had got her conker from. "My dad got it for me and he soaked it for a week in vinegar to make it hard."

"Dads pull some dirty tricks!" said Alfie as he went and met his mother and Eddie at the school gates.

Alfie helped his mother make the spaghetti bolognese for tea. He enjoyed cooking; he liked to stir the meat and press the garlic into the cooking pot. He liked to dish up and eat as well but he had perfected the art of disappearing when it was time to wash up. He didn't want hands as soft as his face! Mothers were soft; boys were tough! Eddie the Labrador loved it when it was spaghetti bolognese on the tea time menu, because there was always some left for him to finish off in his bowl from the scraps. He licked his lips and wandered off to slump in front of the settee.

Alfie watched television after reading his homework book

out loud to his dad who helped him with the hard words. Alfie was yawning and his mum put him to bed and gave him a big kiss goodnight. She closed the door so that the landing light just shone through the small gap. Alfie snuggled down.

*

The sunbeam shone straight through the porthole into Alfie the explorer's face and woke him up. The ship's bows could be heard to thump into the big waves as it steamed along. Breakfast was served in the ratings' mess and Alfie the explorer joined the crew for a breakfast of bacon, eggs and black pudding. A chap needs a walk on deck after a breakfast like that, thought Alfie as he went out of the door into a surprising hard wind that chilled him to the bone and sent him scuttling back inside.

The captain had invited Alfie up to the destroyer's command centre and wheelhouse. The view was spectacular from the windows of the wheelhouse and Alfie watched as the captain and officers went about their duties.

Visibility was dropping as the ship sailed into the gathering storm in the Bay of Biscay. The forecast was being updated for the worst and the captain ordered his men to prepare for the expected gales of up to force ten.

Even though it was quite a large ship, the destroyer started to lurch about and Alfie felt like he riding a bucking bronco. He held on tight as the waves broke over the bows of the ship and sent water along the grey painted decks before washing off the side.

The radio operator called the captain on the bridge and told him that he was receiving a very weak distress call from a French trawler which was sinking about twenty miles away.

The captain called up the French Coastguards and reported the trawler's position. The weather was too bad for an aircraft to be launched and no other ships were as near as the destroyer.

The captain plotted the position and set in a course to get to the trawler. He ordered full steam ahead and the destroyer crashed even harder into the waves which were whipped up by the now force ten gale. The radar showed the position of the sinking trawler and then all of a sudden it disappeared when they were about two miles from it.

The captain's frown got deeper as he looked at his radar screen; he hoped that he wasn't too late. Then an emergency radio beacon started bleeping. The lookout reported seeing a light in the gloom off the port bow. All eyes were strained in that direction and through the waves they saw a bright orange inflatable life raft with a small light on top. The raft was bobbing violently up and down in the huge waves.

"Rescue stations!" ordered the captain and the crew wearing bright orange life jackets threw a scramble net over the side of the ship.

So that they could get close enough to pick up the fishermen in the life raft the ship had to go upwind and then drift alongside the raft in the calm water it created in the destroyer's shelter. In the storm it was a very dangerous manoeuvre, but the captain wanted to save the men's lives and the risk had to be taken. The destroyer took a terrible battering as it turned sideways on to the waves. The life raft was brought alongside and the four trawler men scrambled up the nets to the safety of the destroyer.

Alfie and the crew covered them with blankets and gave them steaming hot mugs of tea to help them warm up. They then all went down to see the ship's doctor who looked after them. The trawler men were all very grateful to the captain and never seemed to stop saying *"Merci, merci"*.

The ship ploughed on through the storm and after a few hours the wind started dropping and the waves died down. The captain dropped anchor off the French port of Brest where the trawler men were offloaded into a small launch and taken to the harbour. Alfie the explorer had gone with them as he could speak French. The grateful fishermen insisted that he wait by the docks for ten minutes as they disappeared and came back with a case of French Champagne for the captain and crew who had saved them from drowning. Back on board the captain ordered his men to open the bottles and the corks flew – pop! pop! went the corks and the crew all had one glass of Champagne each.

# Chapter Twelve: Pipe Down!

"Come on, Poppet. Wake up, sleepy head," said his mother. Alfie slowly opened his eyes and felt under his pillow to find a French champagne cork. His drawer was getting full up with items from his night time adventures. Alfie wondered how long he could keep finding things. When he was older he would open a museum to his travels, he decided. But not yet.

On his way to school Alfie walked by a big yellow JCB tractor digging a hole in the pavement beside the road. The area was all coned off and Alfie and his mum had to cross over the road to get past. Alfie fancied driving a digger one day, when he was grown up.

School passed fairly quickly that day and in no time at all Alfie was walking back home again with his mum. The JCB had dug a deep long trench and a man was working in the bottom tidying up the trench bottom with a shovel.

They were almost past the road works when there was a big whoosh and the tooth on the digger's bucket cut into a water main and water shot out with great force, knocking the workman in the trench off his feet. Just as he fell over, the water caused part of the trench's side to slip on top of his legs and he was trapped. He shouted for help and the man on the digger quickly climbed down to see if he could pull the man out.

The water was rising and try as he could the driver could not free the trapped man. The water soon covered the man's waist and it carried on rising. Alfie's mother ran to the nearby telephone box to dial 999 for the fire brigade. Alfie stood looking around to see what he could do to help. Next to the trench was a compressor and road drills that the men had used to cut the tarmac. Alfie noticed a spare thick yellow air line that was coiled up beside the machine. He ran round and dragged the pipe towards the trench and passed one end to the driver who put the air pipe to the trapped man's mouth. The water carried on rising and soon it was above the trapped man's head. He managed to breathe through the tube for ages as the firemen worked quickly to turn off the water main and pump the trench out.

They lifted the workman carefully out of the trench and he was taken to hospital by ambulance. He managed to thank Alfie for saving his life before the ambulance took him off.

The JCB driver was so pleased with Alfie that he showed Alfie all the controls on his digger. He even said that, at the weekend, he would let Alfie have a go at digging the hole that was needed in a field down the road for Mr Appleton the farmer.

Alfie got home thinking that he had had a real adventure already. He had only been home for twenty minutes when the local newspaper telephoned his mother. They were phoning to ask if they could send a reporter and photographer to get the full story for their paper of how Alfie saved the man in the trench with his quick actions.

Alfie's mum agreed, and he was very excited. Alfie posed with his mum and Eddie for the pictures and he explained in great detail how he helped save the day.

That night Alfie was tired out as he went to bed. He was looking forward to being in the local paper.

"Night, night, you little hero," said his mother as she tucked him up and gave him a big wet kiss.

\*

The destroyer slipped quietly into Portsmouth harbour, past the old round sea forts and down the estuary. The dockside was a hive of activity as naval ships lined the docks, having maintenance carried out and being loaded up ready for their next voyage. The destroyer was guided into its berth by a small powerful tug that churned up the water as it pushed the warship sideways into a tight space on the quay, between a mine sweeper and an aircraft carrier.

Alfie the explorer thanked the captain for a memorable trip and he was soon on the dockside helping the sailors to load up a lorry with the Inca treasure and the Spanish Conquistadors' armour. Two hours later Alfie the explorer and his precious cargo were backed up in the yard of the British Museum, unloading.

The curators flocked around the packing cases and it was like Christmas as they opened each case in turn to a background of many OOHS! and AHHS! of appreciation. Details of all the contents were noted down and photographed. Alfie the explorer had to show the Museum Chief Curator on the map where the various treasures had been found.

Alfie the explorer was soon at the Royal Explorers Club, and over tea and cakes he told his fellow explorers of his discoveries. They had arranged a special evening with Alfie the explorer as Guest of Honour and, after dinner, he would give them a lecture on his discoveries and his adventures.

That night for the second time in several days Alfie the explorer was dressed in a dinner jacket and bow tie. The audience of prominent worthies clapped him in as he was introduced by the Society's president. The dinner was soon served and Alfie the explorer told them all about how he had found the treasure by solving the puzzle of the statues and he showed them samples of the Inca gold and silver and the Spanish Conquistadors' armour. He told them of his encounter with bandits on the train to Buenos Aires and how his ship had hit a growler iceberg on its crossing to Gibraltar.

He rounded off his account with the story of how the destroyer he was on from Gibraltar ended up saving a French Trawler's crew in a force ten gale. "All everyday stuff to a member of the Royal Explorers Club," he said as he sat down to tumultuous applause.

Members of the club congratulated him for his enthralling lecture and got him to sign autographs on the printed dinner menu. Alfie the explorer was famous.

*

"Look, look, Alfie, you're famous!" said his dad as he dashed into Alfie's bedroom waving a copy of *The Daily Bugle*. There on the second page was a picture of Alfie and his mum and Eddie and a story. The headline was: ALFIE NELSON SAVES DROWNING MAN IN TRENCH.

Alfie was so excited that he almost forgot to look under his pillow. When he did, it was to find a printed dinner menu from the Royal Explorers Society and guest of honour was Alfred Henry Nelson, Discoverer of the lost city of Machu Picchu and the Inca treasure.

Alfie put the menu in the drawer and got dressed for school.

That day at school prayers the headmaster called Alfie up on to the stage to praise him for his actions in saving the man. The school clapped and Alfie swelled with pride.

Lucy the Conqueror sat next to Alfie in class and every time he looked she was smiling at him. "Weird," said Alfie. But really he liked her and later on that afternoon he held her hand under the desk. Perhaps girls aren't so bad he thought. But no kissing! Yuk!

That night Alfie slept like a baby but he didn't remember dreaming about anything in particular. Was this the end of his adventures? We hope not!

# Chapter Thirteen: Take your pict

Today was Saturday and Alfie waited at the window looking out down the street. He jumped for joy when the big yellow JCB digger pulled up in front of his house. Alfie's dad came out to see the digger and he walked down the road behind it as Bill the driver gave Alfie a lift on it to Mr Appleton the farmer's field.

The farmer opened the gate and showed the driver where he wanted the trench digging for the foundations for a new grain silo. Alfie held the tape measure as the driver measured the various dimensions and knocked pegs in to show the outline of the foundations. Alfie's dad chatted to the farmer as the JCB revved up the engine and started to claw out the earth between the pegs. Alfie sat beside Bill the driver on his own little seat and watched as the various levers were pulled and pushed. After about an hour Bill said, "Right, young Alfie, time for you to have a go." Alfie was proud as could be, he was going to drive the digger.

Bill heaved Alfie onto his lap so he could squeeze into the driver's seat, and showed him which levers to pull and push to move the digger's arm and bucket. The engine revved as Alfie pushed the lever down to get the bucket's teeth to bite into the dirt. Then he pulled it towards him before curling the bucket, so that it filled up with the loose earth. He eased the lever to the side and swung the full bucket to the side before tipping out the earth in a heap by the side of the trench. As the earth tumbled out of the bucket, Alfie's dad, who was watching, shouted out "Oi!" and pointed to the earth pile.

Driver Bill looked out and his jaw dropped. There on the side of the heap was an earthenware pot about the size of a biscuit tin and out of it was trickling, bronze and copper coins.

Farmer Appleton, Alfie's dad, Alfie and Bill the driver stooped and picked up the coins.

"Well I'll be blowed," said Bill. "Must be several hundred of them, Roman I think."

Farmer Appleton said that he had heard that this field had been used as a camp in Roman times. Indeed he had occasionally picked up the odd coin when he had been ploughing the field next door.

They carefully picked up all the coins and put them back into the pot. On Monday Alfie's dad took them to the local museum. The curator counted them and split them into several sorts before giving Alfie's dad a receipt for them. The curator told the authorities about the find and a date was set to have an inquiry to decide if they were treasure trove. It was possible that the finders could have a big reward.

Alfie's dad told him all about it when he got home. Alfie and his dad then told farmer Appleton about the inquiry over a cup of tea and a cake in his front parlour.

After tea and an Eccles cake. Alfie went to inspect the trench and he noticed a small coin sticking out of the dirt that they had missed. He picked it up and took it to the farmer who told him to put it in his pocket and keep it safe as a reminder of the day he found a hoard of Roman coins.

When Alfie got home he put the coin in his drawer with his other treasures. He was now collecting treasures from his day time adventures!

He studied the small coin in bed and noticed that it had an Emperor's head stamped on one side and a name on the other side – Hadriana Augustus. Hadriana, thought Alfie, sounds like a girl's name.

Eddie jumped up on his bed and snuggled down beside Alfie; he only did it when he was cold. Alfie didn't mind so long as he had enough room to stretch out and it was like having a hot water bottle in the bed.

*

Alficus the Roman commander pulled his toga tightly around him as he and his black dog Eddicus walked along the hillside. It had been years since they had left home to keep order in Britannia, it was now 122AD. Alficus had been fighting the northern tribes called Picts and he was fed up with having to keep them out of the Emperor Hadriana Augustus's Empire.

The light of dawn was showing across the hillside as he ordered his centurions to parade for duty. Today was a special day and the Emperor was in Britannia on an inspection visit. Alficus was wary because he knew that the Emperor looked into everything.

Alficus had spent most of his time protecting the great wall that was being built to keep out the Scottish Picts. The wall was virtually finished and his men were now on guard in small forts all the way along the top of what they were calling Hadrian's Wall. A horn sounded to announce the arrival of the Emperor, Hadriana Augustus. He was riding a horse with a column of centurions marching behind a solid gold eagle on a tall pole. Alficus had heard that he only walked or rode a horse; he never went in a chariot or carriage.

The Emperor dismounted and Alfie bent down on one knee and bowed his head. "You have done well," said the Emperor. "Come with me on a tour of inspection."

They walked around the battlements and Alficus was relieved that everywhere was neat and tidy. The Emperor decided to walk along the front of the wall to check that he was not paying for half a job. He walked so fast that Alficus and Eddicus had a job keeping up with him. After a while they came to a small stream surrounded by trees. The Emperor asked Alficus to get him some water to drink from the stream as he loved fresh highland water. Alficus collected some water in his helmet and took it back to the Emperor, who was sitting with his back to a tree.

All of a sudden a Pict dashed out of the woods. He looked fearsome with his body dyed with blue berries and his wild locks of hair. He had a large knife upraised and he was bringing it down towards the Emperor. Eddicus snarled and jumped up, clamping his jaws round the Pict's arm which held the knife. The Pict howled with pain and dropped it in the grass. Alficus knocked the Pict over and he rolled into the stream. The Pict looked around himself hurriedly and, realising his mission had failed, quickly ran away. Alficus drew his sword and stood protecting his Emperor and soon centurions were running to help him from all directions.

Alficus urged the Emporer back to safety behind the wall whilst the centurions chased the Pict away.

The Emperor was so grateful that he had been saved that he ordered a silversmith to hastily make Eddicus a solid silver collar which he presented to Eddicus that evening. Alficus the commander was presented with a map showing an estate that the grateful Emperor had given to him for his bravery. The estate was in a select part of Italy called Northern Tuscany. Alficus kneeled and kissed his Emperor's hand in gratitude.

*

Alfie woke up with Eddie's paw in his hand and the dog was looking at him like he had a screw loose. Alfie looked under his pillow and found his map of land in Italy written in Latin. He nearly fell over when he found a grand silver collar with the name Eddicus engraved on it. Eddie had been there too,

but how? Then Alfie realised that Eddie had gone to sleep on the bed with him, so he must have come too!

## Chapter Fourteen: Alfie's Big Foot

The magistate walked into the county courthouse and sat on a grand carved wooden chair behind a polished oak topped bench. Alfie and his dad sat down when the clerk of the court told them to, and the magistrate declared the case of the coins found at Top End Farm to be open.

Alfie listened as the magistrate said that the case was to decide if the hoard of coins found were to be declared treasure trove. Alfie sat and listened as the farmer, Mr Appleton, and Bill the driver gave evidence as to how they had found the coins. Alfie was pleased that he got a mention as being a finder, as did his father.

The magistrate decided that the hoard had been hidden by someone who had intended to recover it but had not and then as no owner was likely to be found, he declared it to be treasure trove and the property of the Crown.

The expert from the museum was called to take the stand and he was asked to state as accurately as he could the value of the total find. The courtroom was hushed as people strained their ears to hear what he had to say. "Fifteen thousand pounds, Sir, as some of the coins are very rare," he said.

The magistrate ordered that the hoard should go to the museum and that the finders be paid a reward for finding it.

Mr Appleton, Bill, Alfie and his dad nearly fell off their chairs when the magistrate awarded them three thousand pounds each as a reward for finding the hoard of coins.

They found it hard not to whoop with joy as they left the

quiet courtroom. Once outside they all went down to the Dog and Duck and sat in the garden with drinks all round. Alfie had a diet Coke and a packet of smoky bacon crisps.

Alfie's mum came to join them with Mrs Appleton and they all celebrated their good fortune.

Alfie and his dad had six thousand pounds between them. They talked about it that night at home as to what to do with it. Alfie's dad said that they should have a holiday and that Alfie could have a new bike. Alfie wanted a computer and electronic games but his dad and mum said that he must save the bulk of his money in his savings account for when he was older. Alfie's dad then gave him a lecture about saving and interest rates which went over Alfie's head. Alfie could already picture the bike he wanted, it had got gears and lights and an electric siren with different noises from police cars to fire engine bells. He was looking forward to cycling to school through the park; it is just what boys my age do, he thought.

He yawned and his dad said that it was late and that all good little boys should be in bed by now. He always says that, thought Alfie as he dragged his pyjamas on and sleepily brushed his teeth. Eddie dropped down in his basket beside the bed and started snoring like a rumbling earthquake. Alfie's head hit the pillow and he was fast asleep.

*

Alfie the mountain climber was looking up at the peak of Mount Everest in the Himalayas. He could see the snow-capped summit in the distance and he was working out the best way to get to the top. The peak was 29035 ft (8850 metres) high and was on the border of Tibet and Nepal.

Alfie and his team of climbers and Sherpa porters had double checked all the equipment and they set off up the first gentle slopes at the bottom of the mountain. The weather was brilliant sunshine and Alfie the mountain climber was pleased that they were getting such a good start to the expedition. He knew that by the time they got to the top it would be 40 degrees below freezing and the icy winds could blow them off the mountain. They trekked on, climbing up through the snowy slopes. It was a slow and arduous task as they had to feel each step they took with their poles in order to check that the snow would hold their weight. The men were all roped together and had metal crampons on their boots for grip.

The climber at the front had just turned round to share a joke with the man behind when he fell through the snow into a crevasse hidden by the fresh snowfall. He plunged down and started dragging the other climbers with him. They all fell on their backs and dug their ice axes in to stop themselves sliding down into the crevasse. The climber was dangling on the end of his rope and all the men strained and pulled him back up out of the crevasse. This was standard stuff for a mountaineer, but they still all laughed with a combination of nervousness and relief at a successful rescue.

The crevasse was bridged with a lightweight ladder and the climbers all edged over the gap, one at a time. The snow got harder as they got higher and after a while they decided to make camp. It was still light, but they knew the importance of being properly set up before nightfall – and getting a good night's sleep. The Sherpa porters put up the tents and, after their meal, the climbers all settled down for the night.

They had been asleep for several hours when Alfie thought that he heard a noise outside. It sounded like a moan. He opened the tent flap to see a giant hairy ape-like man who was holding his big size fifteen foot which was bleeding where he had stood on some crampons left outside the tent. Alfie the mountain climber was frightened at first but he looked into the giant's deep brown eyes and saw that the ape-man meant him no harm. He quickly took a bandage out of the first aid pack and wrapped it gently round the huge foot to stop the bleeding. The giant moaned gently and put a big hand on Alfie's head and rubbed his hair. It then stood up and limped off into the night. As Alfie watched the figure disappear into the dark, he suddenly realised that he had just met the Abominable Snowman!

The next morning, Alfie told his companions but no one believed him. And he couldn't prove it as fresh snow had covered the snowman's tracks.

Next day they set off and climbed higher and higher up the mountain, where the air became much thinner. The lack of oxygen made the climb hard work, and they now climbed slower and rarely talked, reserving all their energy for the climb. Some of the climbers got altitude sickness and they made camp to stay behind as Alfie and two other climbers pushed on towards the summit. They had oxygen bottles to help them breathe and they were soon at Hillary Step, the last obstacle before reaching the summit. The climbers strained every sinew as they inched up the last two hundred feet. Their lungs were complaining as they clambered on to the summit, but still they pushed on. They would get their reward for their hard work at the top.

The view was unbelievable! They stood in an awed silence on the roof of the world gazing out into the distance, drinking in the fantastic view. They were on the top of the world, and vast lands stretched out below them. Snowy mountains gave way to green lands, edged by wide expanse of sea and all topped by an endless sky.

Alfie the mountaineer planted a small Union Jack at the highest spot he could see and they all took it in turns to have a photograph taken.

As he looked over to the north Alfie suddenly saw that the weather was changing for the worst. "Let's get going, the weather's closing in," he said.

The three climbers started going down as the wind suddenly picked up and snow flurries whirled around them. They got about three hundred feet down the mountain when they could

hardly see a hand in front of them. Alfie was in front leading the way with the other two climbers roped thirty feet apart. Alfie knew that somehow they must get down quickly or they could die. He looked behind him – he couldn't see either man in the storm, but he could feel them tugging on their rope. It seemed like an impossible task as he could feel the men faltering and struggling behind him. He was wondering whether he should give up and try to pitch a tent in the howling wind when suddenly, he felt a big warm hairy hand on his shoulder – it was the Abominable Snowman. He pulled Alfie by the hand and led him and his companions down to the safety of a hidden cave entrance. He left Alfie at the entrance and disappeared into the snowstorm.

The men stumbled out of the storm into the cave, relieved that Alfie had led them out of the swirling snow and howling wind. They quickly set about warming themselves up and before long had a cup of tea and some hot instant food. Their spirits revived, they congratulated Alfie on finding the cave. Whilst Alfie would have liked to take all the praise, he told the men that the snowman had guided him to the entrance before vanishing into the snowstorm. They laughed at Alfie and said that he had a very good imagination - neither of them had seen anything in the storm. But they said it was a good tale anyway, and that he was just being modest.

Later the storm abated and the climbers made their way down to the base camp. Their companions with altitude sickness were better and were pleased to hear that they had made the summit and had photos to prove it.

That night they all celebrated in a hotel in Katmandu and had a hearty meal before taking a nice hot bath and turning in.

*

Alfie opened his eyes and looked at the sunlight streaming through his bedroom windows. He felt under his pillow and he found a photograph of a mountain climber in full climbing gear at the top of Mount Everest and he stared at the bottom left corner to see a great white hairy ape-like creature waving!

# Chapter Fifteen: The mind reader at 35,000 feet

Alfie dashed past the teacher at the gates, waving goodbye to his mum. He could see his classmates were playing with a football in the playground and he was off to join them.

William passed Alfie the ball and, skilfully dodging a dirty tackle from Tim, he kicked the ball. Lucy who was in goal saved the kick with a particularly good save (for a girl!) and the ball spun away towards a group of big boys from the next year up.

One of the big boys called Butch Grimsdale (The School Bully) picked up the ball and said, "Thanks! Just what I wanted." He pushed past them and walked off with it under his arm, pushing Tim over hard on the concrete ground, and making him cry. What a bully, thought Alfie; he needs taking down a peg or two.

The school bell rang and it was time for lessons. That day the friends discussed what they could do but decided that the bully was too dangerous to deal with.

At lunch time they saw Butch Grimsdale bouncing the ball against the wall. He kept shouting out to the friends, "I've got your ball; I've got your ball!"

Alfie decided that he had had enough and he went over and said, "Please, Butch, can we have it back?"

Butch pushed Alfie over and scratched his knees. Alfie lost his fear of the bully. He stood up and went towards Butch.

Butch was shocked that someone was coming at him. They normally ran away. Alfie, in his fury, ran at him and kicked Butch as hard as he could on the shin. Butch turned and ran away holding his shin and crying in pain because he was a coward at heart. He dropped the ball and Lucy picked it up. They all said that it was the bravest thing they had ever seen. Alfie's class lost all fear of Butch the Bully. For a few days afterwards, when any of them saw Butch in the playground, they called him Butch the Baby, and pretended to cry and limp away holding their shins. He never bothered them again.

After tea Alfie's dad sat down with his mum to discuss the promised holiday. They had got brochures from the travel agent and they started to look at all the places that they could go to. Alfie's mum wanted to go somewhere hot with a nice beach and his dad wanted to relax. They decided on the Caribbean – possibly Antigua, with its 365 beaches, one for each day of the year. Alfie was excited at the thought of flying on a big jumbo jet.

He went to bed that night and the pillows seemed to suck him in like big white clouds.

*

Captain Alfie checked the autopilot on his flight deck and he gazed out of the cockpit window. He welcomed the passengers on board his Boeing 747 jet and he said that they all had to pay attention to the safety demonstration given by the stewardesses. He told them to sit back, relax and enjoy the flight to the sunshine island of Antigua.

Captain Alfie checked all his instruments and sat back to let the autopilot fly the plane. The head stewardess brought him a cup of coffee and a custard cream biscuit. The aeroplane was now cruising at a height of 35,000 feet and was flying above the clouds in bright sunshine. It was so bright that he and the co-pilot put on dark sunglasses. Even though they had radar they still kept a lookout for other traffic that Air Traffic Control warned them about from time to time.

Captain Alfie handed over to the co-pilot and put on his cap and went for a walk among the passengers. People like to see the captain and they asked him lots of questions, like who was flying the plane! After a good long walk up and down he went back to the pilot's seat and took command. The flight to Antigua would take about eight hours; he had done it many times before and basically he just took off and landed manually with the autopilot doing the bulk of the flying.

Suddenly a silver object flashed by his windscreen and took up a position just above and in front of the jumbo. Captain Alfie and his co-pilot were stunned when they realised that it was a flying saucer. They tried to radio the Air Traffic Controllers but their radio didn't work. A blue and red beam of light came from the UFO and it appeared to be scanning the whole aeroplane. Fortunately the passengers couldn't see the UFO as it was in front of the plane. At least his passengers weren't panicking.

The beam scanned the cockpit and Captain Alfie was suddenly transported into the spaceship. He was surrounded by little men who looked like children. One of them touched his forehead with his finger and Captain Alfie felt all sorts of strange sensations as the alien read his mind. He sensed that they meant no harm. He looked about the strange ship and could see very few controls except a big sort of TV screen that showed the outside; he could see the plane and it was still flying properly without him.

After a short while the alien started putting thoughts into Captain Alfie's mind. He suddenly felt that he was very clever and that he could do sums in his head without having to work them out on paper. He noticed that all the aliens had a round silver button on their little chests. The alien read his thoughts and gave him one for himself. The alien told him that it was a signal transmitter and he could use it to get in touch with them

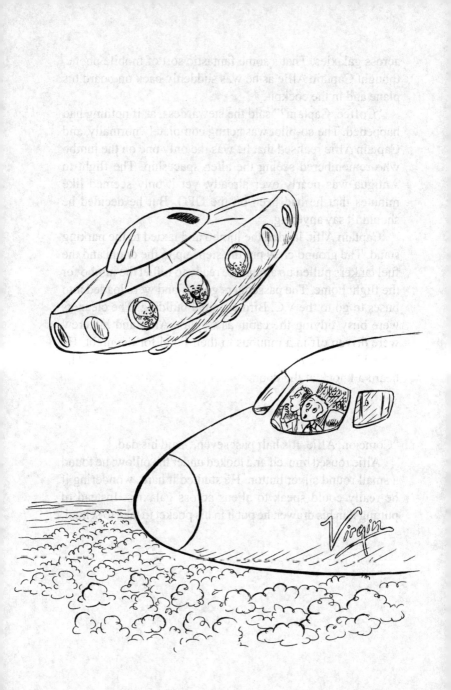

across galaxies. That's some fantastic sort of mobile phone, thought Captain Alfie as he was suddenly back on board his plane and in the cockpit.

"Coffee, Captain?" said the stewardess, as if nothing had happened. The co-pilot was acting completely normally, and Captain Alfie realised that he was the only one on the jumbo who remembered seeing the alien spaceship. The flight to Antigua was nearly over already, yet it only seemed like minutes that he had been on the UFO. But he decided he shouldn't say anything.

Captain Alfie landed the jumbo and taxied to the parking stand. The ground crew put the steps up to the doors and the fuel tankers pulled up alongside ready to refuel the jumbo for the flight home. The passengers got off and were loaded into buses to go to the V.C. Bird terminal building. The cleaners were busy tidying the cabin as Captain Alfie and his crew were driven off in a minibus to their hotel for the night. He would be pleased to get to bed. As he was getting into bed he heard a knock at the door.

*

"Come on, Alfie, it's half past seven," said his dad.

Alfie roused himself and looked under the pillow; he found a small round silver button. He studied it hard, wondering if he really could speak to aliens across galaxies. Instead of putting it in his drawer, he put it in his pocket to take to school.

# Chapter Sixteen: Bright as a button

At nine o'clock the teacher stood by the school front door and rang a small hand bell to tell Alfie and his mates that it was time for their first lesson. Today it was maths and the teacher had written sums up on the board for the class to work out during the lesson.

The classmates of class J4 all sat down and looked at the blackboard covered in sums and groaned. The teacher told them to work out the answers, then bring their work up for marking. If they got stuck they were to put up their arms and she would come and help them.

Alfie wrote down the first sum and looked at it. It was a long sum with multiplying and addition and subtraction. He looked around and all of his mates had their arms in the air. The teacher started to help them when Alfie felt in his pocket and found the silver button from his previous night's dream. He looked at the sum and he could suddenly see the answer. He wrote it down and then he went right down the page and answered every question in five minutes flat.

The teacher was surprised when Alfie marched out to her desk and put his book down for her to mark. She was still helping William to do the first one. "Here let me see, young man," she said in a disbelieving fashion. She was amazed to see that Alfie had finished every one correctly. She gave him a star and said well done. Well done silver button, thought Alfie. He would try an experiment to see how well it worked.

Alfie sat down and he touched Lucy's hand as he held the

silver button in his pocket. She sat bolt upright and started answering the questions as fast as she could write.

Pretty soon the whole class held hands and were answering every question correctly.

The teacher thought that the sums on the board would last the class all the lesson but suddenly she was faced by the smartest kids she had ever taught. There must be a bit of trickery going on, she thought. She decided to write out a very hard sum on the board to test them out. She wrote 27 divided by 9, times 6, plus 7, minus 6. She was just finishing writing the number 6 when Alfie heard himself saying, "Nineteen, Miss!"

The teacher dropped her chalk in surprise at the right answer and turned to see that Alfie hadn't even had to write it down. In fact all the children knew the answer and none had written it down.

She set sum after sum and each one was answered correctly. The bell for the next class rang and the teacher sat down feeling drained as the classmates went to their next class of geography.

The silver button worked in all of Alfie's classes that day and children knew the capitals of Peru, Bolivia, Argentina, Australia, New Zealand and on and on.

The teachers were all talking in the staff room about class J4 and their astounding knowledge. They thought that the children were pulling a stunt and they wanted to get to the bottom of it.

After school Alfie took the silver button out of his pocket and he was surprised to find that it had gone black. He looked at a sum and didn't know the answer straight away but at least he could now remember how to work it out. The button was exhausted.

When Alfie got home he got some metal polish and started rubbing the button. The button got slightly brighter with each rub of the cloth. Alfie felt all clever again but he decided that he had better save the button's power for another time when it could be important. He put the bright silver button in the treasure drawer, rubbed Eddie on the head and climbed in between the clean crisp sheet and the soft duvet and drifted away to sleep.

*

The cavalry horses' hooves clattered as they cantered into the courtyard of the moated manor house. The officer in charge leapt from his horse and banged on the old oak door. "Open up in the name of Oliver Cromwell, the Lord Protector!" A young servant pageboy opened the door to be pushed to one side by the brash young officer.

The officer strode into the drawing room where Lord Alfie, the Lord of the Manor, sat beside the huge fireplace. "What is the meaning of this intrusion?" said Lord Alfie.

"I'm here acting on information that you have a priest taking confessions; we want him. Where is he?"

"You must be mistaken, we've no priests here. Search if you want," said Lord Alfie.

The roundhead officer and his men searched the house but found nothing. They left without saying a word and rode off. After five minutes Lord Alfie pulled at a hidden lever and the side of the fireplace swung open to reveal a priest and two of his parish assistants. The priest and his two men were squashed in like peas in a pod. The priest hole had only been made to take two people really and three was a real pinch.

"You must wait until dark and then leave," said Lord Alfie. The servant boy brought them some meat, bread and cheese to eat and the hungry, wanted men ate like it was their last meal. Lord Alfie did not like to see people persecuted on their religious beliefs. He stood for all that was good in his Manor - the people trusted and respected him for this. Lord Alfie knew that he was constantly being watched by the roundhead sympathisers and he had to be on his guard. He was a royalist at heart and felt that he had to look after his friends, even though Oliver Cromwell was trying to round them all up and chop their heads off, like they had done with King Charles.

The priest and his assistants left after dark and went off to the next safe house on their journey around the county. They had just knocked on the door of a farmhouse in the next village when they were captured by the roundheads and taken to Bedford prison to await the magistrates' trial. Bedford prison was part of the bridge that spanned the river Ouse. The cells were all very damp as the river soaked the foundations and rose up the walls. Lord Alfie knew that they would be tortured to make them confess their crime of being a catholic, before a quick trial and execution.

Lord Alfie got together his most trusted of men and he decided to rescue the priest and his men. He arranged for a large shipment of wine and beer to be sent across the bridge at eight o'clock that evening shortly after the guard had been changed for the night.

The wagon was stopped and searched for traitors as it was crossing the bridge when the guards discovered that it was for Lord Alfred (a known royalist sympathiser), they decided that they would tax it for crossing the river. They took a large barrel of beer and a few bottles of Port wine.

Two hours later, the singing coming from the bridge prison's guardhouse had died down to a few snores and wheezes. Lord Alfie had slipped a sleeping draught into the port and beer, which had clearly done the trick.

Under cover of darkness one of Lord Alfie's men rowed a small boat to the side of the bridge. Lord Alfie gently pushed the guardhouse door open to double check that all the guards were fast asleep. He then walked past them, took a huge brass key off a hook on the wall and unlocked the cells containing the priest and his men. They sneaked out of the prison and down some steps at the side to the waiting boat

below. The boatman rowed slowly and gently away upstream. Lord Alfie was just over the bridge on his way home when he saw the captain of the guard coming for his midnight inspection.

The captain suddenly came running out of the guard room shouting and ringing the alarm bell. Lord Alfie jumped on his horse and, as he rode away, he fired his pistol so as to just miss the captain and break a window next to him. The captain roused some of his men and set off in pursuit of the man who fired at him - as he must have just escaped from the prison. As the captain and his men chased Lord Alfie downstream, a small rowing boat going in the opposite direction was pulling into the riverbank about a mile upstream at Kempston.

There were horses laid on for the priest and his men to escape with. Lord Alfie had doubled back and was there to wave goodbye after the priest had given him a golden cross as thanks. They rode west as fast as they could towards Oxford where a younger brother of the priest would help them.

Lord Alfie got home to Moreteyne Manor and his servant put the horse out in the field, so all looked normal. Lord Alfie then hid the golden cross inside the priest hole by the fireplace in his drawing room. He had just got into his bed when he heard the clattering of roundhead cavalry horses in the yard.

*

The sound of bottles being tipped into the glass collecting vehicle woke Alfie up. How come they are always outside my house at half past seven in the morning, he thought. Alfie rubbed his eyes and felt under his pillow. He pulled out a large brass key that was engraved BEDFORD PRISON.

# Chapter Seventeen: Sniffing around the Park

As they sat having breakfast, the front letterbox rattled as the postman shoved some letters through the opening. Eddie came bounding into the kitchen with a mouthful of letters. "He is a retriever," said Alfie's dad as he wrested the letters from Eddie's mouth. Eddie stood staring at the sweetie cupboard as he thought that he had been very good fetching the letters and he deserved a treat. Mum obliged him.

Alfie's dad opened the first letter and it was a bill, as were the second and the third. Then he noticed that the last two letters were the same shape and size with a grand looking crest printed on the back. Under the crest was printed British Museum. Alfie's name was on one and his dad's was on the front of the other.

They both opened them together and each contained a letter thanking them for their find of Roman coins and a cheque for three thousand pounds each. Alfie, his mum and dad danced around the kitchen table at their good fortune. The same thing was happening at Farmer Appleton's and Bill the digger drivers' house.

Alfie's dad took the cheques and said that he would pay them in at the bank that lunchtime.

Alfie had a quiet day at school and his teacher found that class J4 were not geniuses after all but they could all write the sums down and work them out properly. She decided that she was a very good teacher and that they had all learnt their maths skill from her.

Alfie's mum met him at the school gate with Eddie and they walked home via the park.

They were just laying the table for tea when Alfie's dad came in from the back door. That's funny, thought Alfie, he normally comes in through the front. "Alfie, come into the back garden for a minute, there's something I want to show you," said his dad.

Alfie squealed with delight as he saw a brand new bike with the gears and electric horn propped against the garden fence. He played on it in the garden until dark when his mum called him in for bed. There was another surprise – air tickets for Antigua on Virgin Airlines. Wow!! They were going on holiday too! What a day, he thought.

Alfie lay back on his bed with Eddie and floated away to sleep.

*

Police Sergeant Alfie and Eddie his tracker dog were on patrol in their white and orange police van. The radio crackled into life and the control room asked them to go to number five Willow Road and help to search for a missing child.

Sergeant Alfie put on the blue flashing lights and siren as he speeded towards the house at Willow Road. He quickly parked and went to knock on the door. Before he could knock, a worried Mrs Armitage opened the door and started to tell Sergeant Alfie about her missing daughter Annabelle. She had gone out to play in the park and had not come home for tea. Mrs Armitage found a recent picture of Annabelle and showed it to Sergeant Alfie. She was a pretty little girl with long blonde hair. She was wearing a green jumper and blue jeans. Mr Armitage came back from searching for his daughter but had not found her. Sergeant Alfie asked Mrs Armitage to give him Annabelle's school blazer jacket. He told them not to worry, he was sure that she would turn up and he left in his van for the park.

Once there he told Control where he was and he took Eddie the police dog out of the back of the van. He put a special harness on Eddie and Eddie knew that he was going tracking. He took the school blazer from the van and pressed it to Eddie's nose for him to take a good sniff and pick up the missing girl's scent.

He then started the search by the swings and, after a bit of sniffing around, Eddie started to pull Sergeant Alfie along. Sergeant Alfie followed behind Eddie at a fast walk. Every now and then, the dog stopped and sniffed and went off again. They went right through the park and into bluebell woods. It was starting to get dark and Sergeant Alfie switched on his torch to see where he was going. Eddie led on and on, deeper into the woods.

Suddenly, Eddie started barking and dashed down a slope at the side of the path. There at the bottom of the slope was the missing little girl. She was crying with relief at being found and cuddled Eddie who was giving her big licks. Annabelle told Sergeant Alfie that she had been playing in the park when she decided to pick some bluebells in the woods for her mother as a surprise. She had picked a big bunch when she slipped and fell down the slope by the path. She had badly twisted her ankle and couldn't stand up. She had scratched her face and got mud in her hair.

Sergeant Alfie radioed his Control to tell them that Eddie had found the missing child and he would take her home to her parents. He picked up Annabelle and carried her to the police van and took her home.

Mrs Armitage was so pleased to see them that she made a cup of tea and then tried to scold Annabelle for going off but ended up crying and kissing and hugging her. Sergeant Alfie got Eddie out of the van and Annabelle kissed and hugged him. Best of all, she gave him a large beef bone from her father's butchers shop. Eddie's eyes nearly fell out as he picked up the bone; he enjoyed making friends with the butcher's daughter.

*

There was a thud as the bone hit the floor beside the bed. Eddie jumped down and picked it up, then urged Alfie to let him out into the garden. He went to the flower bed and dug a hole and buried it. Alfie laughed as Eddie was saving it for a later date. He always buries his bones, thought Alfie. The trouble is that he can never remember where he hid them!

No time to lose this morning, thought Alfie, as he dressed and rushed his breakfast down. He was off to school on his new bike. Alfie's dad walked beside him to make sure that he rode properly down the cycle path. Alfie turned on the electric siren and it sounded just like a small police car. As he got to school he dismounted and parked it in the cycle rack. He put on the combination lock and said goodbye to his dad.

Alfie put on his white apron and sat in domestic science class listening to the teacher explaining how to make bread. Soon it was their turn to make it. Alfie carefully weighed out the wholemeal flour and sieved it. He then added a large pinch of salt, made a well in the middle and poured in some warm water with yeast dissolved in it. He held the bowl in his left hand and mixed it with his right. The dough squelched through his fingers as he blended it into a smooth dough. He rolled it into a big ball and dusted it with flour to stop it sticking to the bowl. The covered bread dough was put into a warm cupboard and after about twenty minutes it had swollen to twice its size. The teacher then showed them how to knead the dough, put it into bread baking tins and then in the hot oven.

The smell of the hot bread baking was fabulous and all the class waited in anticipation for it to come out of the oven.

Whilst they were waiting for it to cook, the class had to clear up the kitchen and all the cookware. Alfie enjoyed making the mess but not cleaning up much.

The teacher went to the staffroom for five minutes and left them to it.

Alfie was cleaning the table when William, who was mopping the floor, came up behind him and wiped his legs and shoes with the mop. Alfie turned and pushed William who went backwards, slipped and sat down in the mop bucket. William's knees came up to his nose and his bottom was stuck fast in the large mop bucket. The class laughed as William was helped to his feet by Alfie. William had just stood up when the teacher came in and told them to be quiet as she could hear them down the corridor. All the class were giggling when they saw William had a big wet ring on his trouser bottoms. Poor William sat down on a radiator to dry out. He had learnt not to play about in class.

The bread came out of the oven and the teacher served them a slice each with butter and jam. They all had a nice large wholemeal loaf to take home for their tea and to show their parents how clever they were.

Alfie carefully wrapped his loaf with some tissue paper and put it in his bag. My mum will like this, he thought.

That afternoon his mum came on her bike and collected Alfie from school. They rode home through the park and Alfie put on his siren to warn the world that he was coming. He put his bike in the shed and then he showed his mum the loaf that he had made. He wouldn't let her slice it up until his dad came home and saw it.

"More bread, Mum? Dad?" said Alfie.

Alfie's dad laughed, "It's normally us trying to get you to eat your tea, not the other way round!"

"Perhaps if you cooked the tea every day we would always

have a clean plate!" said his mum.

Even Eddie had a slice of the bread, although he liked his toasted and smeared thickly with margarine.

Alfie went to bed that night with a very full stomach; perhaps he would cook a few meals at home in future, so long as his mum washed up afterwards!

# Chapter Eighteen: Out with a bang?

"Happy Birthday, Alfie," sang his mum and dad, bursting into his bedroom at seven o'clock the next morning. Even though he knew it was his ninth birthday that day, they still took him by surprise. Eddie sat up at the end of the bed looking at the brightly wrapped presents, he liked birthdays too as they usually meant cake.

As Alfie opened his presents his mum was saying to his dad, "Only seems like yesterday when we found him under the Gooseberry bush in the garden, where the stork had left him." Oh yeah, thought Alfie, pull the other one. He knew where babies came from, his biology teacher had told them in class.

He opened the biggest present first and whooped "YEESSSS" at discovering a Radio/CD player for his bedroom table and several CDs (though he thought that they were more to his dad's taste than his.) He liked the stuff currently in the charts, but Eddie liked gentle music to chew bones to. He cuddled his mum and said thanks. Dad gave him a big hug and was about to kiss him when Alfie said that he thought that he was now old enough not to be kissed by his father.

"OK," said his dad, before grabbing Alfie and giving him a big wet kiss on the cheek. He then nipped out the door so Alfie couldn't retaliate.

Alfie dressed for school and ate a huge breakfast of cornflakes and toast. He patted Eddie on the head and went and got his bike from the shed.

He peddled off down Acacia Drive towards school. He rang his bell and waved to Bill the digger driver who was parked in front of Mr Armitage's butchers shop. Bill was eating a large pork pie at eight thirty in the morning.

Alfie locked his bike up and went into his classroom for the morning registration.

He sat down beside William and was a bit upset when nobody said Happy Birthday to him. They all know, he said to himself. (After all, he had told them all last week!)

Classes progressed and all day nobody mentioned his special day. The afternoon bell for the end of school was just about to ring when there was a knock on the classroom door. "Alfie, get the door will you please," said Mrs Allendale.

Alfie opened the door and was immediately confronted by a clown with a big red nose, huge feet and large trousers held up with red braces. "Happy Birthday, Alfie," trumpeted the whole class. He was whisked outside to the playground where a small marquee had mysteriously appeared that afternoon.

The clown was there with the compliments of Bill's trenchman, Patrick, who Alfie helped to save when the trench collapsed. Patrick was delighted to be able to thank Alfie with a party for him and his class. The table was laid with sandwiches, jelly and drinks and the clown did magic tricks that didn't work but they were really funny.

The teachers and parents all came in and sang Happy Birthday to Alfie just as a huge cake with nine candles was brought in. The candles kept re-lighting every time Alfie blew them out. The clown lifted them off the cake, went outside and put them out in a bucket of water. He then stepped back into the tent with the same bucket and then made out to throw it over the class. They all squealed as the contents of the bucket flew over them. They then realized that it was full of confetti!

The school dinner lady cut the cake into slices and

everybody had a piece. Alfie took three pieces, (one for him and two for Eddie!).

That night Eddie slumped beside the bed with two slices of cake inside him and half of Alfie's piece as well. He was soon snoring loudly and Alfie put cotton wool in his ears to keep out the noise.

Alfie was soon yawning and he turned out the bedside light and drifted away into the warm comfortable bed. His heart was beating slowly like a small drum.

*

Alficus was on the back deck of the Roman galley boat as the time keeper beat on the drum for the galley slaves to row in time to. Alficus was on his way home to claim the Villa in Tuscany that the Emperor Hadriana Augustus had given him for saving his life.

Alficus felt sorry for the slaves; he didn't agree to them being chained up and forced to row. Even though they were mainly prisoners of various Roman war victories, they deserved better. Alficus decided to try to help the slaves. When the Galley reached port, the slaves were changed to row back. Alficus spoke to the prison slave master and bought all twenty of the slaves that had rowed him back to Tuscany. He was after all a rich man and needed workers to help run his estate. He bought several wagons and horses to pull them.

The first thing he did when they were all away from the port was to appoint a foreman to organise his men. He gathered the freed men together and told them that he didn't agree with slavery and that all the men would work for wages. The slaves all cheered him and were grateful to have such a man to work for.

They arrived at the estate after five days' travelling. Alficus sat down with each man in turn and wrote out all their details in a book. He found that he had farmers, carpenters and blacksmiths among his men. Each man had to agree to behave and serve him loyally in return for having their freedom after five years' work.

The ex-slaves responded with such loyalty that pretty soon Alficus had the best estate in Tuscany. Every year Alficus bought more slaves with the estate's profits and freed those who had served him loyally. Some of the men wanted to stay as they had never been treated so well. They built homes and settled down, working as free men for Alficus.

One of the freed slaves came to Alficus and suggested that as men were released and able to go back to their own countries, they could start up trading companies to buy and sell goods which they could ship to and from Tuscany. Alficus agreed to give each man enough money as he left to set up in business. Alficus had a business in over ten different countries in as many years.

Romans came from all over Italy to witness Alficus's estate methods and marvel at the work being done by unchained slaves who sung as they worked. They found that the methods could be used on their own farms and that slaves worked better without the whip and didn't run away at the first opportunity.

Alficus sat on the terrace of his villa looking out over his vineyards and listened to the workers singing as they harvested the barley in the fields below. The fountain in the courtyard burbled as the water spurted out of a carved fish's mouth. There was a smell of lavender in the air.

*

Alfie's mother leaned over him and gently shook him awake. Alfie could smell her perfume of lavender soap. That smell transported him back to Tuscany. However it was Saturday and time to go with her to the Beach Café at Sandcastle Bay and see Grace.

Alfie looked under his pillow and found a large ear of barley corn and a link from a chain. He put them in the drawer under his bed and dressed for the beach, perhaps he, Grace and Eddie would have another exciting day.

The wind was whipping across the beach that morning and the sand was flying like small bullets as Alfie got there with his mother. Usually he helped put up the umbrellas on the outside picnic benches and stocked them with napkin and sauce dispensers. Today though, Grace's dad asked him to put out the wind breakers all round the seating area. It was like wrestling with the sails of *The Labrador*, thought Alfie, as a gust of wind nearly took the windbreak out of his hands. He battled fearlessly with the elements for a good twenty minutes until the job was done.

Alfie's mum had got everything ready for opening the café. The coffee was hot and the smell of grilled bacon and sausages soon brought people into the café for breakfast.

Eddie sat outside the café out of the wind with his nose going like a hoover, smelling the rich aromas of the breakfasts being cooked. He knew that Alfie would come and share a bacon sandwich with him before they went exploring along the beach.

Alfie appeared and Eddie went into the "I'm a poor starving dog" routine. Alfie obliged him with a bacon rind and Eddie was restored, until Grace arrived with a sausage and mustard sandwich.

"It's not very nice today," she said, "Let's go over the dunes at the back where it's sheltered." Alfie agreed and Eddie tagged along, sniffing at every post on the way.

All along the ridgeline of the dunes there were old wartime bunkers which had been boarded up or filled in. Alfie and Grace knew them all but as they walked along they noticed that the wind had exposed a corner of a steel door in a dune. "I don't ever remember seeing a bunker there," said Alfie as he started to dig it out with his bucket and spade. Grace started to help and even Eddie joined in. (He thought that they were looking for rabbits!) After about ten minutes digging the door was fully exposed.

Alfie got a bit of wood and levered against the door frame. The door squealed loudly as it opened for the first time in over fifty years.

Inside the door a set of concrete steps led down into the darkness. Alfie peered in but couldn't see a thing in the pitch black. He nipped back to the café and took the front lamp from his bike.

"Hurry up," said an impatient Grace. The intrepid explorers edged carefully into the old bunker. The walls were green with the damp and a musty smell hung in the air. Old tables and chairs lined the room and a large sign on the wall said BLUE AREA CONTROL. At the rear of the room was another door with STOREROOM marked in big red letters on it. Alfie and Grace pushed on the door and when it opened, they could see that it was lined with racks storing wooden boxes - dozens of them.

Alfie flicked his torch onto the side of one of the crates and noticed the stencilled black sign WD HANDLE WITH CARE. "Wait a minute there's more writing," said Grace.

Alfie brushed the dust from the side of the crate and shone his torch to read E, then X, then P, then L, then O, then S, then I, then V, then E, then S.

"Explosives!" they both shouted and they turned round and ran out of the bunker up the steps and into the daylight. They blinked at each other, called Eddie (who had his nose down a rabbit warren sniffing) and raced the distance back to the café. They ran into the café and started to tug at Alfie's mum's apron to tell her what they had just found.

"Look, I've got a lot of people to serve, tell me in a minute!" said a busy Mrs Nelson. Alfie thought that his mum could normally earwig three conversations in a room and serve customers at the same time. So why could she not listen to what two excited children were trying to tell her?

Alfie waited patiently with Grace and Eddie until the customers were served. "Now then, tell me what's going on," she said.

Alfie explained what they had found and on her tea break (What was the hurry, children exaggerate, thought mum) she went with them over the dunes to the bunker. She took one look at the racks of explosives and ran back to the café to phone the emergency services.

Within twenty minutes the back of the beach road was covered in emergency vehicles with blue flashing lights. Barriers were erected and the dunes were cleared of people (and dogs).

A large blue four-wheel drive lorry with Naval bomb disposal experts drove right up to the entrance of the bunker and the men cautiously went inside. They were so taken aback with the large amount of munitions, that they asked the police to clear everybody back over a quarter mile radius of the find.

The Navy team slowly and gently started clearing the ammunition boxes away, stacking them into a deep trench in the dunes that Bill the digger driver had been asked to dig for them. Sightseers came from miles around to look from the nearby café at the clearance work.

Sky TV sent a news crew down to report on the find and Alfie, Grace and Mrs Nelson were interviewed about the bunker and its munitions.

Several times that day a siren was sounded and the explosives were safely detonated in the trench. Alfie and Grace covered their ears at the loud noise, the ground shook and a cloud of sand whooshed high into the air. Eddie was hiding under the café's decking when Alfie found him. "Perhaps I ought to explain to him that he's a brave gundog," said Alfie to Grace. Grace cuddled Eddie and gave him a big kiss to make him better.

Grace's dad and Alfie's mum were rushed off their feet by the crowd of onlookers (even Alfie and Grace helped with clearing the tables) and by closing time that day they had sold out of every cake, sausage, pie and portion of chips that they had.

Even when they were locking up people were still arriving. Grace and her dad went off to the late night cash and carry to fetch some more stock for the next day. Alfie, Eddie and his mum went home.

"Had a good day, son?" said his dad.

"Oh, it was quiet," said Alfie, smiling.

"He's pulling your leg," said his mum and went on to explain to his father what had happened at the beach that day.

"Into bed, you," said Mum as she drew back the covers for Alfie. "Time to get a good night's sleep so you are ready for more adventures tomorrow."

Alfie smiled to himself as he thought of the adventures that lay ahead of him tonight.

ISBN 1-905203-20-9

**Available on your next Virgin flight
and from all good bookshops**

ISBN 1-905203-21-7
Out October 2005 - order now-

ISBN 1-905203-22-5
Out October 2005 - order now-